Enid Blyton

The Rilloby Fair Mystery

Illustrated by Eric Rowe

AWARD PUBLICATIONS LIMITED

For further information on Enid Blyton
please visit *www.blyton.com*

ISBN 978-1-84135-729-4

First published 1950 by William Collins Sons & Co. Ltd
First published by Award Publications Limited 2003
This edition first published 2009

Published by Award Publications Limited,
The Old Riding School, The Welbeck Estate,
Worksop, Nottinghamshire, S80 3LR

11 2

Printed in the United Kingdom

CONTENTS

1	First Day of the Holidays	7
2	Snubby Enjoys Himself	16
3	An Unexpected Meeting	25
4	Great-uncle Tells His Story	34
5	Diana Has an Idea	44
6	Snubby Says Something Silly	52
7	Snubby in Difficulties	60
8	Off to the Fair	70
9	Good Old Barney Again!	79
10	An Interesting Afternoon	88
11	Barney Comes to Supper	97
12	Plans!	108
13	Diana Does Her Bit	116
14	At the Fair Again	125
15	A Nice Afternoon – and a Sudden Ending	134
16	A Morning at the Castle	143
17	The Fair Moves to Rilloby	153
18	Snubby Enjoys Himself	161
19	More Doings of Snubby	170
20	A Most Exciting Find	180
21	Midnight at the Castle	188
22	A Night Out For Snubby	197
23	It's All in the Papers!	207
24	The Police Arrive	215
25	Quite a Lot of Talk!	223
26	The Second Green Glove	233
27	Sunday – and Monday	241
28	Things Begin to Happen	250
29	Burly Is Very Clever	260
30	The Mystery Is Solved	269
31	All's Well!	277

1

First Day of the Holidays

"Morning, Mum! Morning, Dad!" said Roger, and ruffled his father's hair as he passed him and dropped a kiss on his mother's curls.

"Don't do that, Roger," said his father impatiently, smoothing his hair down. "Why are you late for breakfast? And where's Diana?"

"Can't imagine," said Roger cheerfully, helping himself to an enormous plateful of porridge. "Asleep, I suppose."

"Never mind," said his mother. "It's only the second day of the holidays. Roger, you can't possibly eat all that porridge – with sausages to follow."

"Oh, jolly good," said Roger, sitting down in front of his great plateful. "Any fried onions with them?"

"Not at breakfast-time, Roger. You know we don't have onions then."

"I can't imagine why not," said Roger. He began to eat his porridge, craning his neck to read the back of his father's newspaper.

As the newspaper was folded in two, the reading matter was upside down for Roger, and his father glanced at him irritably.

"Roger! What are you screwing your head round like that for? Have you got a stiff neck?"

"No – only just reading that exciting bit in the paper about the dog that . . ."

"Well, don't. You know it's bad manners to read a paper when someone else is reading it," said his father. "Don't they teach you manners at school?"

"No. They think we learn them at home," said Roger, cheekily.

Mr Lynton glared over the top of his newspaper. "Well, then, perhaps I'd better teach you a few these holidays," he began. And just at that moment Diana burst into the room, beaming.

"Hello, Mummy! Morning, Dad! I say, isn't this a heavenly day – all daffodils and primroses and sunshine! Gosh, I do love the Easter hols."

"Get your porridge, dear," said her mother. "Roger, you haven't taken all the cream, surely?"

"No, there's a spot left," said Roger. "Anyway, it won't hurt Diana to have plain milk. She's too fat."

"I'm not! Am I, Mum?" said Diana, indignantly.

Her father gave an exasperated click. "Sit down, Diana. Eat your porridge. If you must be late, be late quietly. Breakfast is at eight o'clock – and it's now half past!"

Mr Lynton gathered up his newspaper, put it beside his wife's place, and went out of the room.

"What's the matter with Dad this morning?" asked Diana. "Why is Dad so miserable, Mummy?"

"Don't talk like that, Diana," said Mrs Lynton. "There's nothing wrong with your father except that he does like you two to be punctual for meals – and also he's heard that Uncle Robert is coming to stay. You know the dear old fellow bores your father terribly."

"Oh my goodness – is Great-uncle Robert really coming?" said Roger. "Whatever for? And where are you going to put him? Snubby's coming tomorrow, isn't he, and he'll have the only guest-room."

"Well, he can't now – he'll have to sleep in your room," said his mother. "I'll have a bed put up there. I'm sorry, Roger, but it's the only thing to do. Uncle Robert must have the guest-room."

"Oh gosh – Snubby sleeping with me and playing his stupid tricks all the time," groaned Roger. "I shan't mind having Loony in the room, but Snubby's awful."

"I'd very much rather you didn't have Loony sleeping in the bedroom with you," said Mrs Lynton. "He's a very nice spaniel, I know, although he's completely mad – but I do not like dogs in bedrooms."

"Mum! You say that every single time Snubby and Loony come to stay," said Diana. "And you know quite well that if you turned Loony out into the kennel Snubby would go too, and sleep with him there at night."

"Yes, I know," said Mrs Lynton with a sigh. "I don't know which is worse – Snubby or Loony."

Snubby was a cousin of the two children, and owned a black cocker spaniel called Loony, short for Lunatic. Snubby's parents were dead; so he spent his holidays staying with various relations. Mrs Lynton was sorry for him and fond of him, and he came more often to her house than to anyone else's.

"He's coming tomorrow, isn't he?" asked Diana. "I'll order a big bone for Loony today when I go past the butcher's. Dear old Loony. I wonder if he's still mad on brushes. Mummy, last summer hols he took every single brush he could find. He put some of them down a rabbit-hole. We found quite a collection there one day."

Mrs Lynton hurriedly made up her mind that she would warn the household to keep all brushes out of Loony's reach. Oh dear – what with Snubby and Loony and Uncle Robert, it looked as if things would be much too hectic for the next few weeks.

"I wonder what Snubby will say to Great-uncle Robert," said Diana with a giggle, helping herself to sausages. "Oh, Mummy – I just can't see them together, somehow.

Uncle Robert's so haw-hawish and pompous – and Snubby's so mad and idiotic."

"You'll just have to keep Snubby and Loony out of your uncle's way, that's all," said her mother, getting up from the table. "Well, I'm sorry I can't wait for you two any more. I see you've finished up the toast and have begun on the loaf of bread. When you've finished that perhaps you'd like to call it a meal! I cannot imagine how you can put all that away."

"Easy," said Roger, and grinned at his mother as she went out of the room. She smiled back. It was nice to have the children at home again, but it did take a little time to get used to their enormous appetites, careless ways and constant sparring.

Silence fell when Mrs Lynton had gone out of the room. The two munched away hard, gazing out of the window. Daffodils danced at the edges of the lawn, and wall-flowers shook the scent from their velvet petals. Sunshine flooded the garden and the two children felt happy and excited. The weeks stretched before them – no lessons, no rules – only day after day of sunshine and holidays, enormous meals, ice creams – and Loony the dog to take for walks.

"Heavenly," said Diana, coming out of her daydream. Roger knew what she had been thinking, and he agreed.

"Yes, great," he said. "I wonder how

Loony will get on with Sardine."

Sardine was their big black cat, so-called because of her great fondness of the tinned fish called sardine. The checkout girls at the local supermarket were always astonished at the amount of tinned sardines Mrs Lynton bought – fancy a family eating as many sardines as that! But it was Sardine the cat who ate them all, and waxed fat and sleek on it.

"I should think Loony will give Sardine a frightful time," said Roger, scraping out the marmalade pot.

"I'd be surprised if Sardine didn't hold her own quite well," said Diana. "Let me have a scrape of that marmalade, Roger. Don't be a pig."

"I wish Great-uncle Robert wasn't coming," said Roger, handing over the marmalade pot. "I wonder why he's coming. He doesn't usually come in our hols. It's the last thing you'd think he'd want to do, considering he thinks all children are perfect pests."

"Diana! Haven't you two finished yet?" called Mrs Lynton from upstairs. "Come along. I want you to help me with Snubby's bed. I'm putting the playroom divan into Roger's room. Roger, come and give me a hand with it."

"Never a moment's peace!" said Roger with a grin at Diana. "Come on. Let's give a hand."

They tore upstairs, falling over Sardine as they went. The big black cat fled up in front of them, tail in air, green eyes gleaming wickedly.

"Sardine! Do you still lie on the stairs, you wicked cat?" shouted Roger. "You be careful tomorrow, or Loony will get you if you don't look out!"

"Loony'll get you if you don't look out. Loony'll get you if you don't look out!" chanted Diana, and skipped into Roger's room to help her mother. Sardine was sitting on the windowsill there, her long tail waving from side to side.

"What have you two been doing to make Sardine so cross?" asked her mother.

"Well, I like that! She was lying doggo on the stairs waiting to trip us up!" said Diana, indignantly.

"Lying catto, you mean!" said Roger with a chortle.

"Oh, Roger – you sound like Snubby when you say things like that!" said his mother. "Diana, make Roger's bed while he and I bring in the divan."

They were busy that day, preparing for Great-uncle Robert and Snubby – what an odd pair! Great-uncle Robert was so old and polite and pompous, correct in every way, and Snubby was so very much the opposite, cheeky, idiotic and unexpected in all he did. Mrs Lynton had quite a few qualms when she thought of them in the house together.

As for Loony, he would probably drive the old man mad. All the same, Loony was a darling, and Mrs Lynton, like everyone else, had fallen under his spell. Dear, silky-coated, melting-eyed Loony. There was probably only one person in the household who would regard Loony with bitter dislike – and that was Sardine.

At last the two rooms were done. The guest-room looked nice and bright and clean. Flowers arranged by Diana stood on the dressing-table, bright yellow daffodils matched by the yellow towels hanging by the basin.

Roger's room looked different, now that it had the extra divan in. It wasn't very big anyhow, and looked very crowded now, with the divan and an extra chair. Mrs Lynton also added an old rug in one corner for Loony to sleep on.

"Oh, Mum! What's the good of that?" said Roger. "You know where Loony always sleeps – on Snubby's feet."

His mother sighed. It looked as if these holidays were going to be just a little bit too exciting. She was quite right – they were!

2

Snubby Enjoys Himself

Snubby was pleased to be going to his cousins' home for the holidays. He liked Mrs Lynton, their mother, and he quite liked Mr Lynton, though he was secretly afraid of his sudden tempers. It would be good to see Diana and Roger again.

His luggage had gone in advance. He only had a small bag with him – and Loony, of course. He was now waiting for the train, a snub-nosed, red-haired, freckled boy of twelve. He whistled tunelessly as he waited, and Loony pricked up his ears as he always did when his beloved master made a noise of any sort.

The train came in with such a roar and rumble that Loony was startled. He jerked away in alarm, and rushed into the waiting-room, where he cowered under a seat.

Snubby followed, indignantly. "What do you think you're doing, idiot, rushing away like that! Anyone would think you'd never seen a train before. Come here!"

The train gave a piercing whistle, and Loony cowered back still farther. Snubby had a job to get him to move.

"Look here – the train will be gone before we've caught it if you don't look out!" shouted Snubby, exasperated. "Come *out*, I tell you. What's come over you?"

He dragged poor Loony out at last, lumped him into his arms and staggered to the train. The guard was already slamming the doors.

"Hey you – get in quickly!" yelled the man. "Train's just going!"

Poor Snubby had no chance to choose his compartment carefully as he usually did. He liked a completely empty one, so that he could occupy each corner in turn and look out of any window he liked. There was no time to look into even one compartment now. He wrenched open a door, threw Loony in, and fell in himself, landing on hands and knees. The door slammed behind him, and the train moved off.

Loony retired under the seat. Snubby glared at him. "Idiotic dog! You nearly made us miss the train!"

He got up and dusted himself down. He looked round the compartment. Only one other person was there, thank goodness.

The one other person stared at Snubby in annoyed surprise. He was an old man with a head of silvery-white hair, a real mane.

His eyes were a faded blue and he had a small pointed beard, also very white.

"My boy," he said. "It is most inadvisable to leave so little time for catching a train."

"I've been waiting for twenty minutes," said Snubby, indignantly. "Here, Loony, come on out. You'll get filthy under there."

Loony appeared, his tail well between his legs. The old man looked at him with dislike.

"Dogs!" he said. "I think they should travel in the guard's van. They always smell. And they scratch themselves in such an objectionable manner."

"Of course dogs smell," said Snubby, sitting down opposite the old man. "It's a nice smell, a doggy smell. So is a horsy smell. And I like cow's smell too. And as for . . ."

"I don't think I want to discuss smells," said the old man. "I do not like the smell of dogs, and I do not like the way they scratch themselves."

"Loony never scratches," said Snubby, at once. "A dog only scratches when he's got heaps of fleas. I keep Loony jolly clean. Brush him every single day, and . . ."

Loony put himself into a peculiar position and began to scratch himself very hard indeed, making a thumping noise against the floor of the carriage.

Snubby pushed him crossly with the toe of his shoe. "Shut up, you idiot dog. Didn't you hear what I just said?"

Loony looked up politely, and then began to scratch himself again. The old man looked disgusted. "Do you mind taking him to the other side of the carriage?" he said. "Bearing in mind your remark about dogs only scratching themselves when they have a large number of fleas, I don't feel too happy about having him in quite such close proximity."

"What's that mean?" asked Snubby obstinately, not moving. "I tell you, he hasn't got fleas, he's never—"

"I don't think I want to discuss fleas," said the old man stiffly. "Well, if you won't move your dog, I must move myself. But I must say that children nowadays are not remarkable for their good manners."

Snubby hastily removed Loony to the other side of the carriage, feeling rather ashamed of himself. The spaniel tried to climb up on the seat, but the old man looked so very disapproving that Snubby changed his mind about letting him.

Loony fortunately went to sleep. Snubby undid his case and took out a paperback book. He settled down to read. The old man looked to see what Snubby was reading. The book had a most lurid cover and an extraordinary title. It was called *Spies! Spies! Spies!*

Snubby curled himself up, lost to the

world. The old man was astonished to see such a peculiar title.

"What is your book about?" he asked at last.

Snubby thought that was a silly question, considering that the book's title was plainly to be seen.

"It's about spies," he said. "Stealing old maps and plans and things like that."

The old man gazed at Snubby and then made a curious remark. "Spies! I never thought of that! It might have been spies."

Snubby looked up, astonished. "Funny old fellow!" he thought. "What's he talking about now?"

"It's strange you should be reading a book about old documents being stolen," said the old man. "Because I've just left a place where there's been a theft of that kind. Terrible, terrible!"

Snubby stared at him. "What exactly was stolen?" he asked.

"The letters of Lord Macaulay, maps of the county of Lincolnshire, and the correspondence between Lady Eleanor Ritchie and her sister," said the old man, shaking his head solemnly. "And the old recipes of the Dowager Lady Lucy, and . . ."

This was all Greek to Snubby. He began to think the old man was pulling his leg. All right, he could do some of that too!

"And I suppose the pedigree tables of all

the dogs went too, and the letters written by Lord Popoffski," he said, solemnly and sympathetically.

Now it was the old man's turn to stare. "Ah – I see you don't believe me," he said with dignity. "Well, let me tell you this, young man. The thief got into a locked room without unlocking it. He got into a room with every window fastened and didn't unfasten one. He left no fingerprints, he made no noise."

Snubby didn't believe a word. He looked disbelievingly at the old man.

"Well," said the old fellow, "that's a strange story, isn't it? Too strange for me. I've left the house where it all happened, and I'm not going back there. I don't like thieves who go through locked doors. Do you?"

Snubby put down his book. If there was to be a bit of storytelling, well, he would do some too.

"Funny you should tell me this, sir," he said earnestly. "I'm running away too. I've unearthed a Plot, sir, a very sinister Plot."

"Good gracious!" said the old man, alarmed. "What kind of a plot?"

"Sort of nuclear bomb plot," went on Snubby, enjoying himself. "They tried to get me – and they very nearly did."

"Who tried to get you?" asked the old man, amazed.

"Sh!" said Snubby, mysteriously, looking all round the compartment as if he thought "They" were listening. "It's the Green Hands – surely you've heard of that gang?"

"No. No, I can't say I have," said the old man. "Who are they?"

"An international gang," said Snubby, enjoying himself more and more, and marvelling at his powers of invention. "They've got the secret of some special bomb, and I stumbled on it by accident. They captured me and wanted me to work for them."

"What – a boy like you?" said the old man.

"They can use boys," said Snubby. "For experiments and so on, you know. Well, I didn't want to be blown to bits, did I?"

"Good heavens!" said the old fellow. "This is incredible. You should go to the police."

"I'm running away," said Snubby, sinking his voice to a whisper. "But they're after me – the Green Hands. I know they are. They'll track me down. They'll get me in the end."

"But this is unbelievable!" said the old man, mopping his forehead with a big white silk handkerchief. "First I stay in a house where thieves go through locked doors and fastened windows and now I travel with a boy hunted by – by what, did you say – the Green Hands? Do they – do they have green hands?"

"They wear green gloves," invented Snubby, wildly. "Beware if you ever see any-one wearing green gloves, won't you? Man or woman."

"Yes. Yes, I certainly will," said the old man. "My poor boy – have you no parents to look after you?"

"No," said Snubby, telling the truth for the first time in five minutes. "I haven't. I'm fleeing to the country to stay with my cousins. I hope the Green Hands don't track me there. I don't want the whole lot of us blown up."

"Good heavens! Incredible! The things that happen these days!" said the old man. "Take my advice, my boy, and go to the police."

The train drew to a stop. Snubby looked out casually, and then suddenly leaped to his feet, startling the old man considerably.

"Golly! This is my station! Here, Loony, wake up! Stir yourself. Goodbye, sir – and I hope you catch your locked-door thief."

"Goodbye, my boy. We've had a most interesting conversation – and take my advice, go to . . ."

But his words were lost in the noise of the engine and the slamming of the door. Snubby was gone and so was Loony. The old man sank back in his seat. Well, well, well – what was the world coming to? To think that even a young boy could be mixed up in such extraordinary plots. Most alarming.

"Nobody's safe these days!" thought the old man gloomily. "It's all most alarming."

3

An Unexpected Meeting

Snubby arrived on the platform very hurriedly, fell over Loony and sat down with a
bump. A squeal of laughter greeted him.

"Oh, Snubby!" cried Diana's voice. "You
always fall out of a train! Hello, Loony!"

Loony flung himself on Diana in a mad
bound, almost knocking her over. He barked
and yelped, pawing her ecstatically. She had
to push him off at last.

"No, Loony, no more. Get down. Snubby,
tell him. He's just as loony as ever, isn't
he? I say, Roger's sorry he couldn't come
and meet you, but he's gone to the next
station to meet Great-uncle Robert. Why
you couldn't both come to the same station,
I don't know! I suppose Great-uncle thought
the next one was nearer to us."

"Who's Great-uncle Robert?" asked
Snubby in surprise. "I've never heard of him
before. Surely he's not coming to stay?"

"Yes, he is. Maddening, isn't it, considering it's our hols," said Diana as they walked

out of the station. "He's not a bad old thing, only awfully pompous and polite. Mummy didn't know till yesterday that he was coming. We've had to put you in Roger's room."

"Oooh, good," said Snubby. "Loony will like that."

"Does he still take every brush he can find?" asked Diana. "He was awful last summer hols."

"Yes, he's still pretty bad about brushes," said Snubby. "And mats. And cats too. I say – you've got a cat now, haven't you?"

"Yes. A big black one called Sardine," said Diana. "She's almost a year old, so she's still pretty idiotic at times. I don't know how she'll get on with Loony."

"It'll be a lively household," said Snubby, pleased. "Cats and dogs flying all over the place, and us three, and your old great-great-uncle."

"Only one great," said Diana. "He's Mummy's uncle. Well, there's our house. Loony remembers it, look! He's rushing in at the gate. My word, he'll startle old Sardine – she's basking on the wall!"

Snubby ran after Loony. Loony had already discovered Sardine and was chasing her madly round the front garden, yelping in excitement. Sardine flew into the house, Loony raced after her, and Snubby tore after them both.

Mrs Lynton was amazed to see Sardine flash past her head and land on top of the bookcase. She was even more amazed to see Loony coming in like a streak of black lightning, followed by a shouting Snubby.

"Oh! It's you arriving, Snubby. I might have guessed," she said. "There's really not much difference between you and a tornado. How are you, dear?"

"Hello, Aunt Susan!" said Snubby. "Come here, Loony. Oh, good – Sardine's gone out of the window now. Gosh, so has Loony."

He disappeared at top speed and Mrs Lynton sat down again with a sigh. Peace always vanished when Snubby arrived. There were loud cries from the garden, and finally a scream from Diana.

"Mummy! Here's Great-uncle in a taxi with Roger."

Mrs Lynton got up hurriedly. She wondered what Uncle Robert would say when he found the front garden full of yells and yelps, howls and yowls, and screaming children.

She went into the garden and hissed at Snubby. "Catch Loony at once. Take him away. Go and wash your hands or something!"

Snubby gave her a startled glance. How cross she sounded! He gave a piercing whistle and Loony responded at once. He arrived like a cannon-ball at Snubby's heels, and the two disappeared indoors just as Great-uncle Robert opened the front gate. Diana smoothed back her hair and went to welcome him too.

"So nice to be here at last, my dear Susan," said the old fellow. "Such a peaceful place – far from thieves and wars and spies!"

Mrs Lynton felt astonished. "Oh, we're peaceful enough here, out in the country," she said. "Come along up to your room. You would like a wash, I expect."

"Thank you, my dear, thank you," said Uncle Robert, and followed his niece up the stairs. She took him to the guest-room and put his bag down for him.

"Very nice room," said Uncle Robert. "Very nice view too. Beautiful. Ah – who's this?"

It was Loony. He came nosing into the bedroom, having smelled somebody new. He stood at the door, wagging his black stump of a tail, his long ears drooping like a judge's wig at each side of his head. Uncle Robert looked at him.

"Most peculiar," he said. "There was a dog in the train, in my carriage, exactly like that!"

"Oh, well – black cocker spaniels are very much alike," said Mrs Lynton. "Now you wash, Uncle Robert, and then come down to lunch. You must be hungry."

She went to a cupboard on the landing to put some things away. Snubby was whistling in Roger's room, brushing his wiry hair and making it stand up straighter than ever. He suddenly missed Loony.

"Hey, Loony! Where have you got to?" he said. He went to find him. Ah, there he was, standing in the doorway of the room next but one. He went to get him. Somebody came walking out at the same moment, stepping carefully over Loony, who didn't attempt to move out of the way. He never did if people were stupid enough to walk round or over him.

Snubby stopped in utmost amazement when he saw Great-uncle Robert. He stared as if he couldn't believe his eyes.

Great-uncle Robert stared too.

"Incredible!" he muttered, taking a step backwards and nearly falling over Loony. "You again! What are you doing here?"

"I'm staying with my cousins," said Snubby, horrified to see that the old man in the train had suddenly become Great-uncle Robert. Gosh, this was frightful. That awful story he had told him – about the gang called the Green Hands! Suppose he told Aunt Susan about it, what in the world would she say? She wouldn't understand at all. She would be furious!

"So this is where you were running away to," began Great-uncle Robert. "Do your

29

cousins know why you're here?"

"Sh!" said Snubby desperately. "Don't say a word to anyone. Remember the Green Hands! They'll get you too if you split."

"Split?" repeated Great-uncle Robert faintly, not understanding the word.

"Blab. Spill the beans. Give the game away," said Snubby, urgently. "Don't say a word. Just remember the Green Hands!"

Somebody suddenly banged the old gong in the hall as a signal that lunch was ready, and both Great-uncle Robert and Snubby jumped violently.

"Sh!" said Snubby again, and looked all round him as if he were being hunted.

"I'll remember the Green Hands," said Great-uncle Robert in a stronger voice. "But be careful, my boy, do be careful."

He went downstairs, wiping his broad forehead with his silk handkerchief. He had escaped from one house where thieves made their way through locked doors only to come to another place where there was a boy hunted by the Green Hands. Where should he go next? Incredible, quite incredible.

Up on the landing, half-hidden by the open cupboard door, was a most astonished Mrs Lynton. She had overheard the extraordinary conversation and couldn't understand a word of it. What was all this about green hands and all the shushings and

warnings she had heard? She was filled with amazement.

"What's Snubby up to now? And how does he know Uncle Robert? And what is this talk of green hands?" she thought, shutting the cupboard door impatiently. An agonised yowl made her jump. She opened the door hurriedly and Sardine jumped out.

"Silly cat! Why put your tail in the door when you know I'm going to shut it?" said Mrs Lynton. "You're always doing things like that. There now, I'm sorry I hurt your tail. And just look out for Loony, because I don't want you streaking across the dining-table as soon as you see him!"

Loony was downstairs with the others. He had attached himself to Great-uncle Robert, much to Diana's surprise. He was sniffing round his feet and pawing at his legs in a most friendly manner.

"He's acting just as if he's met you before," said Diana.

"Er – is he?" said Great-uncle Robert, not knowing quite what to say. "Snubby – call him off, will you? I don't particularly want his fleas, you know."

"How do you know he's got fleas?" asked Roger, surprised. "Has he, Snubby?"

It looked as if the conversation was now going to be awkward. Snubby pulled Loony away and shoved him firmly under the table.

"Of course he hasn't got fleas," he said. "You'd jolly well know if he had. Why, a chap at school had a dog that had about three hun—"

Mrs Lynton came in, still looking puzzled. "What are you talking about?" she asked, sitting down at the head of the table.

Nobody told her. She didn't encourage subjects of that sort at mealtimes. Uncle Robert took his place gingerly, looking under the table to see exactly where Loony was.

"What's that noise?" inquired Mrs Lynton, hearing a thump-thump-thump on the floor under the table.

"Oh, just Loony scratching himself," said Diana.

"Oh dear, Snubby – and I hope you haven't brought Loony here with—" began Mrs Lynton.

"No, Aunt Susan, I haven't," said Snubby, hurriedly. "I say – is that chops – and chips – and *onions*!"

The subject was safely changed. Mrs Lynton served the meal, still wondering about such curious things as green hands. She glanced at Uncle Robert. He seemed such a nice, harmless old fellow. What did he mean, whispering about running away and green hands up on the landing with Snubby?

It was really most extraordinary!

4

Great-uncle Tells His Story

After the meal Snubby escaped into the garden with Roger and Diana, Loony at their heels. They all went into the little summerhouse, which faced south and was very warm in the April sun.

"Gosh! It's as hot as summer," said Roger. "I'll really have to take off my jumper. I say – Great-uncle Robert is rather an old stick, isn't he? We'll have to mind our manners a bit now, or he'll get going on the 'good old days when children knew their manners, and were seen and not heard,' and all the rest of it."

"I've got something to tell you," said Snubby, rather awkwardly. "About Great-uncle Robert."

"Go on then – out with it. What have you been doing? Using his hair-lotion for Loony or something?" asked Roger.

"Don't try and be funny," said Snubby. "It doesn't suit you. Listen – I came on the train with him, and I got off at the North

Station and he went on to the South, where you met him. We had quite a lot of – er – conversation."

The other two looked at him in surprise. "You did?" said Diana. "Well – why ever didn't you say so then? Why keep it such a deep, dark secret?"

"Well, you see – it's like this – he told me a silly story about running away from somewhere he'd been staying, because thieves had got through locked doors and stolen papers and things," said Snubby. "Lord Somebody's letters and Lady Somebody's recipes – a lot of awful nonsense. And – well – I told him a story too. I thought to myself, well, two can play at this game, and I sort of let myself go."

"Do you mean you went and fed him some frightful fairytale?" said Roger. "Whatever did you tell him?"

Snubby related the story he had told to Great-uncle Robert, ending with his running away from a gang called the Green Hands, who always wore green gloves. Diana and Roger listened in astonishment that ended in giggles.

"Gosh, Snubby, you really are the biggest fathead that ever lived!" said Roger at last. "What in the world did you go and tell Great-uncle all that for?"

"Well, how was I to know he was your great-uncle?" demanded Snubby. "I didn't know he was coming to stay with you. I got a shock, I can tell you, when I saw him in the guest-room. I nearly passed out."

"You'll get another when he tells Dad the rigmarole you told him," said Roger. "Dad doesn't like fairytales of that sort. He doesn't understand that kind of joke."

"I know," said Snubby dismally. "I've warned Great-uncle not to say a word. He really believes it all, you see. I expect he's terrified of the Green Hands Gang now – just as terrified as he is of the thieves that walked through the locked doors at the house where he was staying."

"Well, he must be a mutt if he believes a word you say," said Diana. "Oh dear, Snubby – you always bring trouble with you. Now don't you go frightening the old man with sinister notes, or drawings of green hands or anything."

"Oooh – that's an idea," said Snubby, sitting up. "Oooh, I say – wouldn't he have a fit!"

"Yes, he would – and the first thing he'd do would be to tell Dad, and you'd get a good telling-off," said Roger.

"That's no go then," said Snubby, who had quite clear memories of one of Uncle Richard's tellings-off. "I don't want to go too far with Uncle Richard."

"You'd better not," said Roger. "He's not in a very good mood so far these hols –

because Great-uncle has come to stay, I think – and what with that, and us, and you and Loony, life seems pretty grim to him at the moment."

"Poor Dad," said Diana. "We'd better keep out of his way."

"It's an idea," said Snubby, making up his mind not to get in his Uncle Richard's way any more than could be helped. "I say – I wonder if Great-uncle will tell his thief-story to Uncle and Aunt."

He did, that very night. They were all sitting in the lounge together, the children playing a game, Mrs Lynton sewing, her husband reading, and Loony having one of his lengthy rolls all over the floor.

Great-uncle filled his pipe and then spoke to Mrs Lynton. "It's really very kind of you, Susan, to have me here at such short notice," he said. "But to tell you the truth I was at my wits' end. I simply had to leave the Manor House."

"Did you, Uncle Robert? Why? Weren't you comfortable?" asked Mrs Lynton.

"Oh yes, quite. Very warm, comfortable house, the Manor House at Chelie," said Uncle Robert. "But there were such extraordinary goings-on, you know."

Mrs Lynton looked rather startled. The children nudged one another and laid down their cards. "Now it's coming," whispered Snubby.

Mr Lynton put down the evening paper. "What extraordinary goings-on?" he asked. "Surely not much can happen in a house like that, that's more a museum than anything else."

"It's a place of great treasures," said Great-uncle, reprovingly. "It belongs to Sir John Huberry, as you know, a man who collects rarities of many kinds – in particular old papers, letters and documents."

"Er – hasn't he got some of Lord Macaulay's letters?" said Snubby innocently, remembering what Great-uncle had mentioned in the train.

There was a surprised silence, during which Loony could be heard scratching himself vigorously.

"Shut up, Loony," said Snubby, and poked him with his toe. Loony stopped.

"Well, it's the first time I've ever heard you make an intelligent remark," said Mr Lynton, in surprise. "I shouldn't have thought you had ever even heard Lord Macaulay's name."

"Er – Snubby is quite right," said Great-uncle hastily. "There were some of Macaulay's letters, they were among the stolen articles. Richard, it was the most extraordinary theft. Doors were locked. Windows were fastened tightly. There was no skylight or other way into the room where these papers were kept. And yet one night thieves got in, took the whole lot, and vanished the way they came – through locked doors or fastened windows! What do you think of that?"

"I think it's rather foolish to make a statement like that," said Mr Lynton. "Thieves can't get through locked doors unless they have a key."

"Well, they hadn't a key," said Great-uncle. "The keys are kept on Sir John's key-ring in his pocket. There are no duplicates in existence. What is more, the doors showed no fingerprints of any sort."

"The thieves wore gloves," said Mrs Lynton.

"Green gloves," said Snubby, before he could stop himself.

Great-uncle looked extremely startled. Mrs Lynton stared at Snubby, puzzled. First it was green hands, now it was green gloves. What did he mean?

Mr Lynton took no notice of this remark. He just put it down to Snubby's usual silliness. "Well, Uncle Robert," he said, picking up his paper again, "all I can say is, if that's what you ran away from – the idea of thieves going through locked doors – it wasn't very sensible of you. You should have stayed to try and find out who stole the papers. Why, if your hosts didn't know you well, they might think it was you, as you ran away."

"I hardly think so," said Great-uncle, on his high horse at once. "No, my dear Richard, that is quite unthinkable. Quite."

"I expect it was vagrants or tramps," said Mrs Lynton soothingly.

Great-uncle gave a most unexpected snort. He looked scornfully at Mrs Lynton. "My dear Susan! Do you think a vagrant or a tramp would know what papers were valuable and what were not? This thief knew exactly what to take."

"Well, I've no doubt the mystery will be solved sooner or later," said Mr Lynton, opening his paper again. "I imagine if the thief is as clever as you say, he'll try his hand somewhere else."

"He's already tried it three times," said Great-uncle. "Sir John told me. He thinks it must be the same thieves because each time they apparently passed through locked doors quite easily."

"Well, I'll believe somebody can go through locked doors when I see them," said Mr Lynton dryly.

"Great-uncle – do you think the thief will steal papers again somewhere?" asked Diana. "I'd like to read about it, if he does. Would it be in the papers?"

"Oh, yes," said Great-uncle. "It's always in the papers. I think I've got a report of the last theft in my bag. You can go and get it, if you like."

Roger sped upstairs with Loony at his heels. Loony always went upstairs with everybody if he could, and then tried to get in their way going down again, either by getting between their legs, or hurling himself on top of them as they went down. There was a thunderous noise after a minute or two, and then a crash and a yelp.

"Oh dear," said Mrs Lynton. "Are you hurt, Roger?"

Roger came limping in followed by a saddened Loony. "I've smacked him," he explained to Snubby. "He did his cannonball act at me and sent me flying down the stairs. He's loonier than ever. I've got the paper. Where's the burglary reported, Greatuncle?"

Great-uncle found the report. It wasn't much more than a few lines. The children read them eagerly.

Then Diana noticed an advertisement nearby and pointed to it.

"Look," she said. "There's a notice about a fair held in the same town. I wonder if Barney and Miranda were there."

"Is this the Barney you told me about – the boy with the monkey that had the adventure with you last summer holidays?" asked his mother. Roger nodded.

"Yes. He's awfully nice, Mum. He leads a peculiar sort of life, you know – going from fair to circus and circus to fair, earning his

living with Miranda, his monkey. She's a darling."

Mrs Lynton looked doubtful. "Well, I don't like monkeys," she said. "But from all you have told me, Barney seems a nice boy, though a strange, roving kind of character."

"I wonder if he's at the fair advertised here," said Diana, looking at the notice again. "Look, Roger – it lists the names of all the performers – the main ones, anyway: Vosta and his two chimpanzees, Hurly and Burly – what lovely names; Tonnerre and his elephants. Shooting gallery in charge of the famous marksman, Billy Tell—"

"Short for William Tell, I suppose," said Snubby, grinning. "Go on."

"Hoopla stalls, roundabouts, swing-boats – no, it doesn't say anything about a boy with a monkey," said Diana, disappointed. "Though perhaps they wouldn't mention him, really – he wouldn't be one of the chief performers."

"Anyone got his address?" asked Snubby. Nobody had. Barney was a very bad letter-writer, and the children had not heard from him since Christmas.

"Come on, let's finish our game," said Roger, losing interest in the paper. "No, you can't get on my knee, Loony. Go and play with Sardine – a nice little game of spit-and-hiss, or growl-and-snap. You'll like that!"

5

Diana Has an Idea

A day or two went by. Great-uncle tried to settle down and go on writing what he called his memoirs, which Roger said was another name for nodding over a pipe.

Snubby had settled in at once, as usual. He was perfectly at home, and Roger's usually neat bedroom now always looked exactly as if a whirlwind had just passed by.

"If Snubby doesn't mess it about, Loony does," Roger complained. "I'm tired of keeping my shoes and bedroom slippers and stuff in a drawer so that Loony can't get them."

"So am I," said Diana. "And I do wish he wouldn't drag all the mats in a heap and leave them on the landing or in the hall for people to fall over. I nearly broke my ankle twice yesterday. As for poor Great-uncle Robert, he's so scared of falling over mats or brushes or shoes left about that he walks like a cat on hot bricks – lifting up his feet very gingerly indeed."

44

Roger laughed. "Oh dear — that lunatic dog put half a dozen brushes into the pond this morning, and two of them were Great-uncle's. Snubby told him he supposed Mum was washing the brushes in pond-water because it was good for them — and he believed him!"

"There's Loony now, barking at Sardine, I suppose," said Diana. She leaned out of the window. "Loony, Loony! Shut up! Haven't you learned by now that once Sardine is up on the wall you can't get her off. *Shut up!*"

Her mother's voice came floating up from the garden. "Diana! Stop yelling out of the window like that. Your Great-uncle is trying to work."

"That means Loony's woken him up from a doze," said Diana, pulling her head in. She put it out again. "Mum! Mum! Shall I do the flowers this morning?"

"Will you stop shouting out of the window?" called back her mother, while Great-uncle Robert flung down his pipe in exasperation and stood up. He would go for a walk! What with dogs barking and children yelling, and now his niece yelling too, the house was unbearable. Yes, he would go for a walk!

But at the sight of him appearing in coat and hat with a stick in his hand, Loony flung himself on him in delight. A walk!

People with hats and coats on meant only one thing – a walk! Loony snuffled round Great-uncle's ankles, thrilled, and then rolled over on his back, doing what Snubby called his "bicycling act", riding an imaginary bicycle upside down!

"You are not coming with me," said Great-uncle firmly. "I don't like you. You can only do two things well, and I don't like either of them. You can bark louder than any dog I know, and you can scratch yourself more vigorously."

But Loony meant to come with him. He kept so close to Great-uncle's ankles all the way to the gate that he almost tripped him up. "Home!" said Great-uncle sternly. "*Home.*"

"Woof," said Loony, and sat down expectantly, exactly as if Great-uncle had said "Bone", not "Home." The old man tried to open the gate quickly and slip out without Loony – but Loony was up to that game. He was out in the road with Great-uncle at once, dancing round him maddeningly.

The old man lost his temper. "Snubby!" he yelled. "Call this dog of yours. *Call him*, I say. Do you hear me, boy?"

A woman opposite came over to Great-uncle. "I'm so sorry," she said, "but may I ask you not to shout and not to let your dog bark so much? Your shouting and his barking have kept my baby awake half the morning."

Great-uncle was really exasperated. He walked off down the road, thumping the pavement with his stick.

"I kept her baby awake. What rubbish! And calling Loony my dog! I wouldn't own him for a thousand pounds."

But it certainly looked as if he did, because Loony kept faithfully with him during the whole of the walk, occasionally half-disappearing down a rabbit-hole, but always coming back. Poor Great-uncle.

He bought himself a paper and came back, reading it as he walked. He suddenly stood still and gave an exclamation. Loony sat down beside him and looked at him. What was this old gentleman up to now?

Loony hadn't any use for him really, except to snatch a walk with him now and again.

"Look at that!" said Great-uncle. "Another robbery – same kind of thing – and same way of going about it. Locked doors again! Extraordinary!"

He showed the report of the new theft to Mrs Lynton when he got back. The children crowded round in interest.

"See?" said Great-uncle, pointing to the paragraphs with a beautifully clean and polished nail. "Another robbery. Rare and valuable papers again. And not a trace of the thieves. Doors locked and windows bolted. And yet the things are gone. There's something strange about all this."

"Green Hands," whispered Roger mischievously behind him. Great-uncle turned sharply, but Roger's face was innocent.

"Can I borrow the paper, please?" asked Diana. "Thanks awfully."

She took it to the summerhouse and the three of them pored over it. Diana looked rather pleased with herself. "I've discovered something," she announced to the others. "Have you?"

Roger considered. "No. What?" he asked.

"Well, you know the first paper we saw, the one Great-uncle brought with him and let us read?" said Diana. "Do you remember the bit about the fair?"

"Yes. What about it?" said Roger.

"There's nothing about a fair in this paper."

"I know. I've looked," said Diana. "But did you notice what the first paper said about the fair – where it was going to next? It said it was going to Pilbury. Pilbury. Does that ring a bell?"

"Gosh, yes," said Roger at once. "This theft is at Pilbury. I see what you're getting at. Either the fair goes to a place where there are rare papers to be stolen – or somebody in the fair makes inquiries at each place they go to, to see if there are any in the neighbourhood worth stealing."

"That's what I meant," said Diana. "Let's find out if the fair was actually at Pilbury when the papers disappeared, shall we?"

"Yes. Though I must say we're rather jumping to conclusions," said Roger. "It's probably sheer coincidence."

"I bet it is!" said Snubby. "Just like Diana to think she's spotted something clever!"

Diana gave him a push. "Get out of the summerhouse if you're going to talk like that. Go on! If you're not interested, you needn't be here."

"I *am* interested," protested Snubby. "And don't shove me like that. If you want a shoving match you know who'll win. You won't anyway. And all I said was—"

"If you say it again, out you go," said Diana, getting angry. "I'm tired of you

49

today, Snubby. You've hidden my socks, I know you have, and you left my bedroom door open so that Loony could take my mats again. And now just look at Loony. He's got somebody's brush again. It's Great-uncle's hairbrush this time."

Snubby ran to get the brush away from Loony, who at once regarded this as a wonderful game and danced away down the garden, flinging the brush up into the air and catching it in his mouth.

Diana turned to Roger. "Roger, there may not be anything in my idea at all. Let's find out first whether the fair is at Pilbury. And then let's try and find out where it's going to next and see if a theft of rare papers is reported from there too."

"It's quite an idea, Di," said Roger. "We'll bike over this afternoon – it's not more than ten miles away. We'll leave Snubby behind. I'm getting tired of him."

So they said nothing of their plans to Snubby, but got out their bicycles without his seeing and had a look to see if the tyres were all right. Yes, they were.

They set off after lunch, creeping off while Snubby was arguing with their mother about some missing shoes which she was perfectly certain Loony knew something about. They mounted their bicycles and rode gleefully off down the road. "Sucks to Snubby!" said Roger. "Won't he be wild?

He'll hunt all over the place for us!"

It was a long way to Pilbury, farther than they thought, but they got there at last. They rode all through it but could see no fair. Diana felt a little dampened.

"We'll ask someone," said Roger, and he got off his bicycle. He called to a small boy nearby.

"Hey! Is there a fair in Pilbury, do you know?"

"There was!" called back the boy. "But it's gone. Went yesterday – to Ricklesham, I heard."

"Thanks!" said Roger, and beamed at Diana. "Well, it was here – and now it's at Ricklesham. We'll just see if there's a robbery there next. Then we'll *know* your idea's got something in it. I say – this is rather exciting, isn't it!"

6

Snubby Says Something Silly

Snubby was most annoyed with the other two when they came back. "Where have you been? You beasts, you've been for a bike ride and didn't tell me!"

"Well, you were so jolly unbelieving in the summerhouse we thought we'd go off alone," said Diana. "Sucks to you, Snubby!"

"Whatever's the matter with Loony?" asked Roger, staring at the spaniel in surprise. "Why is he looking so dismal? He didn't even come rushing to meet us."

"He's in trouble," said Snubby. "So's Sardine. They chased your mother's ball of wool all round the lounge and didn't have the sense to see it was joined to a jumper she's knitting. They undid the ball for about a mile of wool, rolled it out to the kitchen, and almost into the pond. Aunt Susan's awfully cross. She smacked poor old Loony so hard that he went under the sofa for half an hour, and she tried to smack Sardine but she escaped."

"Just like a cat!" said Roger. "Poor old Loony."

"You go and eat up Sardine's dinner," said Diana encouragingly to Loony.

"He wouldn't touch sardines if he were starving," said Snubby. "Where have you been, you two?"

They told him. "So you see, the fair's gone to Ricklesham now," said Roger. "And now we'll just wait and see if any burglary occurs there."

"I wish we could hear from Barney," said Diana. "He might know some of the people in the fair. He's been all over the country now in fairs and circuses and shows."

"I'd like to see old Barney again – and dear little Miranda," said Snubby, who had a very soft spot for the small monkey belonging to Barney. "Is it any good writing to Barney's last address?"

"We did that," said Roger. "No answer came at all. We'll have to wait till he writes to us himself."

A strange dog ventured into the garden. It went out again at top speed as Loony hurled himself at it, yelping madly. "He's feeling better now," said Snubby, looking at Loony. "His tail's got a wag again."

Loony disappeared into the house, his little tail wagging. He came out again with the brush from the sitting-room fireplace.

"Look at that!" said Roger, exasperated.

"I'm always carrying brushes about now – putting them back in their places. Loony, you're dippy."

He and Diana went in with the brush. Snubby went off to the summerhouse with a book. But Great-uncle Robert was there, smoking his pipe.

"Oh, sorry, sir," said Snubby, and began hastily to retreat.

"Quite all right, my boy. Come along in," said Great-uncle. "There's plenty of room for two. I want to talk to you."

Snubby never liked to hear that a grown-up wanted to talk to him. It usually meant a ticking-off of some sort. He sat down with a sigh.

"About this gang of yours," said Great-uncle in his rather pompous voice. "This – er – Green Hands Gang – wasn't that what you called it? Have you heard anything more about them? Or was it possibly a little invention of yours?"

Snubby considered. He didn't really want to give up his lovely idea of a Green Hands Gang that wore green gloves. On the other hand, it wouldn't do to work up Great-uncle Robert about it, because he might be foolish enough to say something to Uncle Richard. Then the fat would be in the fire. Uncle Richard wouldn't see that a silly pretend didn't matter. He would call it a lie, and treat it as such. And Snubby knew that he wouldn't be let off lightly.

"I think the gang have lost track of me," said Snubby at last, deciding that would be the safest thing to say. "I haven't heard a word from them since I've been here," he added truthfully.

"Really?" said Great-uncle, eyeing Snubby in a way he didn't much like. "Er – perhaps you think the gang have bigger fish to fry? Other things that are more important than you?"

Snubby blinked. Was Great-uncle getting at him? A sudden thought flashed into his mind and was out in words before he could stop it.

"Yes, I think you're right, sir – and I think you'll hear of their activities next at Ricklesham!"

"Ricklesham!" said Great-uncle, surprised. "Why Ricklesham?"

Snubby now wished he hadn't spoken so quickly. He fidgeted uncomfortably on the wooden seat.

"Don't know, sir. Just a hunch. You see, if you knew that gang as well as I do, you'd sort of know where they were going to – to – operate next."

"Bless us all!" said Great-uncle, staring at Snubby. "I don't know what to make of you. Talking of gangs and how they operate – and looking just a dirty, untidy boy with the most disgusting fingernails I ever saw."

That was a nasty jab. Snubby took a hurried look at his nails. Everybody was always worrying him about them. Why couldn't they mind their own business? He didn't sneer at their clean nails – why should they sneer at his dirty ones? He got up.

"I'll go and clean my nails, sir," he said, pleased at having thought of such a good excuse to get away before Great-uncle asked more searching questions about the gang!

"A very good idea," said Great-uncle. "And while you're about it, wash behind your ears and see if you can possibly reach the back of your neck."

Snubby fled. Nasty, sarcastic old man! Snubby brushed his nails hard with the nail-brush and thought darkly that it would be rather nice to have a real gang to frighten people like Great-uncle Robert.

Diana called to him from her room. "Snubby, is that you? Come here a minute."

He went into Diana's room. She and Roger were sitting on her bed with a map spread out between them.

"What's that?" asked Snubby.

"It's a map with Ricklesham on it," said Diana. "We thought we might as well see exactly where it is in case we want to go over to the fair. It's about six miles off. We'll take you with us next time if you behave yourself."

"Gosh – look at Snubby's nails! He's

56

cleaned them!" said Roger, astonished. "You turning over a new leaf, Snubby?"

"Shut up," said Snubby, feeling quite ashamed of his spotless nails. "Great-uncle's been on at me about them. I say – I said rather a silly thing to him."

"Well, that's nothing new," said Roger. "What did you say this time?"

"He began asking me in a sneering sort of voice about the Green Hands Gang," said

Snubby. "And when I said I hadn't heard a word from them, he said in a horrid scornful voice, 'I suppose they've got bigger fish to fry!' And I said yes – they might be operating next at Ricklesham."

There was a moment's silence. Diana and Roger stared at Snubby in dismay.

"Well! You're a bigger idiot than I thought you were," said Roger at last. "Suppose there *is* a robbery at Ricklesham, what's Great-uncle going to think? That it is your silly Green Hands Gang, and you are mixed up in it. And he'll most certainly split on you and tell Dad."

"I know," said poor Snubby, looking very downcast. "I thought of all that afterwards."

"You're crazy," said Diana. "Here we are on the track of something exciting and you go and blab about it to Great-uncle, and mix it up with your idiotic fairytale."

"Perhaps there won't be a burglary at Ricklesham," suggested Snubby hopefully. But that didn't find favour with the others either.

"That's right. Pour cold water on our ideas now," said Diana. "Tell us we're wrong. Make out it's silly to—"

"I'm not, Diana, I'm not!" cried poor Snubby, feeling that whatever he said would be wrong. "I'll believe anything you tell me, really I will."

"Shall we let him go with us if we go to

Ricklesham, or not?" said Roger grimly to Diana.

"We'll see," said Diana. "Any more fat-headedness on his part, and we don't tell him a thing."

Snubby departed to find Loony, feeling very subdued. He fell over on the stairs, and Roger and Diana heard him rolling down, yelling.

They grinned. "That's Sardine again," said Diana. "She always lies in wait for Snubby on the stairs."

"Do you really think there'll be a burglary at Ricklesham?" asked Roger, folding up the map.

"Well – not really," said Diana. "I did feel it was a sort of hunch, you know – but it's a bit far-fetched, actually, isn't it? I don't suppose anything will happen there at all."

"We'll watch the papers," said Roger. "And what a thrill it will be if we see Ricklesham in the news!"

7

Snubby in Difficulties

Three or four days went by. Each morning the three children took the paper after the grown-ups had finished with it, and pored over it.

But Ricklesham was never in the news. It was most disappointing. And then suddenly it was!

Mr Lynton was glancing down the paper one morning, when something caught his eye. He read it quickly and then spoke to Great-uncle Robert.

"Uncle," he said, "here's a bit of news for you. Didn't you have something to do with the arranging of some old seventeenth-century documents – I've forgotten what they were – for the Forbes-King Collection?"

"Yes. Yes, I did," said Great-uncle. "A very fine collection that was – most interesting old letters. Why, what does it say about them?"

"They've been stolen!" said Mr Lynton. The three children sat up in excitement.

"Stolen!" echoed Great-uncle. "No – have they really? Where from?"

"They were on loan to a Mr Curtice-Knowles at Ricklesham House," said Mr Lynton. Diana gave an exclamation, Roger kicked her under the table. Snubby looked anxiously at Great-uncle.

"Ricklesham House! Ricklesham, did you say?" said Great-uncle Robert in a faint voice. "Good heavens! Ricklesham!"

He looked at Snubby. Snubby had said that the Green Hands Gang might operate at Ricklesham next and lo and behold, what had it done but steal valuable old documents there? Great-uncle did some rapid thinking. Then that meant – yes, it must mean – that the Green Hands Gang that Snubby was afraid of was the same one that was mixed up with the continual theft of precious documents!

"It must have been that very gang that came into Chelie Manor House when I was there, and stole all those papers," thought Great-uncle Robert. "Fancy that boy being mixed up with them. Most extraordinary. I'll have to have a long talk with him about all this. Really, the police should be told."

Snubby wouldn't look at Great-uncle. He was terrified that he would suddenly ask him awkward questions. Fortunately Mrs Lynton plunged into the matter, and asked several questions.

"But Richard! Do you think that it's the same thieves who went to Chelie Manor House when Uncle Robert was there? Does it say anything about locked doors? Did the thieves go through fastened windows and locked doors again?"

"Yes. Apparently it is just as mysterious a theft as the others," said her husband. "There is a small room set apart at Ricklesham House for these old and rare papers, and they are displayed in glass cases. The door to this room was locked, of course. The windows are not only safely fastened, but also barred, so the paper says."

"And yet the things were stolen!" said Mrs Lynton. "It certainly sounds very mysterious. The police must be very puzzled."

Great-uncle took the paper and read the report very carefully. There was no mention of a Green Hands Gang. How on earth did Snubby know that there was going to be a crime committed at Ricklesham? He lifted his head to have another look at Snubby. But Snubby had gone.

He had mentioned to his aunt in a low voice that he didn't want any more breakfast. Could he go, please?

"Don't you feel well, dear?" began Mrs Lynton, but seeing that Snubby's cheeks were the same fiery red as usual, she felt there was nothing seriously wrong. So she nodded, and Snubby slipped away, thankful that Great-uncle was buried in the paper.

There was an excited meeting in the summerhouse that morning. Snubby, Diana and Roger rushed there as soon as their jobs were done. Loony rushed too, sensing the excitement.

"Roger – Great-uncle kept on and on looking at me at breakfast-time," said Snubby, as soon as they were safely in the summerhouse. "I know he's going to ask me awkward questions. I don't want to meet him at all. Say you don't know where I am, if he asks you."

"Well, we can't tell a lie, if we do know where you are," said Diana. "But we'll do our best not to give you away. It serves you right for talking too much. Now, of course, Great-uncle will believe in your silly Green Hands Gang all over again, because of this upset at Ricklesham."

"I know," groaned Snubby. "Loony, go and sit outside on guard. On guard, do you hear? And you jolly well know what that means. Bark if you see anyone coming!"

Loony thumped his little tail on the ground, as he sat himself down in the sunshine. He knew what "On guard" meant all right. Of course he did. He barked loudly at once, and Snubby, in a great flurry, squeezed himself under the seat in the summerhouse, while Diana and Roger sat just above, their legs hiding him.

But it was only Sardine arriving. She had seen Loony and wanted to have a game. So she came walking up the path, waving her tail in the air as usual, black and sleek and purring.

Loony knew now that her purr meant "Friends! Don't chase me!" Just as she knew when he wagged his tail, it meant the same.

Still, he had to bark, as he was on guard, and Sardine paused in surprise. She sat down a good way from Loony and began to wash herself. Loony could never imagine why cats washed themselves so much. They were always doing it.

"It's all right, Snubby – it's only Sardine," said Diana, peering out of the summer-house. "Shut up, Loony. You're on guard for people, not cats! Shush!"

Loony stopped barking. Sardine strolled right up to him, purring very loudly. He wagged his stump of a tail. Sardine lay down, stretched herself out on the path and patted his nose with her paw. Loony gave the tiniest bark. It meant "Sorry, I can't play now, but I'm on guard."

So Sardine went to sleep, leaving a crack of one eye open, just in case. Loony also settled down, shutting both his eyes, but listened with his long, droopy ears.

Snubby came out from under the seat, draped with cobwebs and powdered with dust. "That idiot of a Loony," he grumbled.

"Look at me – I'm in a frightful mess!"

"I can't see that you look much worse than usual," said Diana, looking at him. "Come on, sit down again. We really have got something to discuss."

They talked and talked about the affair. They had all read the bit in the paper now. They knew that once again valuable letters had been stolen, and that once again the thief had apparently passed through locked doors and barred windows.

And, more important still, they knew that once again the fair had been in the same district as the burglary. That couldn't be sheer coincidence – it couldn't be chance. The fair, or somebody in the fair, must be connected with these strange thefts. And that somebody must be clever enough to know about rare documents, where they were, and how to get them.

"The two things don't seem to go together, somehow," said Roger thoughtfully. "I mean – you don't associate show people with a knowledge of that kind of thing. You have to be a person like – well, like Uncle Robert – to know about historical documents. You have to have a lot of specialised learning."

"You mean, you have to be an antiquarian," said Diana, showing off a little. "That's what people of that kind are called. Uncle Robert told me."

"Gosh – I always thought an anti – anti-whatever-you-said, was somebody who was against keeping aquariums," said Snubby, surprised.

Roger laughed, "You would! Anyway, it's not anti-aquarium, idiot, it's antiquarian."

"Sounds just the same to me," said Snubby. "I say, are we going to Ricklesham? Do say we are!"

Roger looked at Diana, and they both nodded solemnly.

"Yes," said Roger. "We'll go to the fair, and we'll snoop round and see if we can find out anyone there who's an antiquarian. Then we might be on the track!"

"That's an awfully good idea," said Snubby. "We can put the police on to him at once."

"It won't be as easy as that!" said Diana scornfully. "We—"

Loony set up a tremendous barking again. Snubby dived beneath the wooden seat once more, and Roger and Diana sat close to hide him.

"It's Great-uncle, this time, all right," said Roger. "Keep still, Snubby. We'll do our best for you."

Great-uncle came to the entrance of the summerhouse. He looked in.

"Ah," he said. "I thought I should find you here. I want to talk to Snubby."

"We'll tell him when we see him, Great-

uncle," said Roger politely.

"Your mother said he was here," said Great-uncle.

"Did she?" said Diana. "Is she busy, Great-uncle? Does she want me yet?"

"That was a quick change of subject!" thought Snubby admiringly from behind her legs.

"No. She didn't say she wanted any of you," said Great-uncle. "Do you know where Snubby is?"

"He's not far off," said Roger truthfully. "Loony's never very far from him, you know."

Loony wagged his tail at his name. He was most astonished to see Snubby under the seat, and would have liked to go to him, but every time he went near either Roger or Diana, they pushed him off with a determined foot.

"Do you think he'd hear me if I called him?" asked Great-uncle. "I really do want to speak to him. It's important."

"You could try shouting," said Diana.

Great-uncle shouted, "Snubby! Snubby! I want you! *Snubby!*"

There was no answer, of course, except that Loony barked, and Sardine fled up to the wall.

"Do you think he heard me?" said Great-uncle.

"Er – if he's near enough, he would certainly hear you," said Roger cautiously. "Never mind, Great-uncle. I'll tell him you want him next time I speak to him."

Great-uncle called again, feeling somehow certain that Snubby was not very far away, otherwise why was Loony there?

"SNUBBY! I WANT YOU!"

"Great-uncle! That woman with her baby in the house opposite is looking out of the window," said Diana. "I hope her baby isn't asleep."

"Bless us all! I forgot the baby," said Great-uncle. "The mother will be after me again. Well, you tell Snubby I've been looking for him, will you?"

He went off down the path, and Roger and Diana heaved sighs of relief. "You can come out now, Snubby," said Roger. "He's gone."

Snubby came out, dirtier than ever. "You did jolly well," he said admiringly. "Never told a lie at all, and didn't give me away either. Thanks awfully."

"I don't know how you're going to manage to avoid Great-uncle all day long," said Diana. "It'll be difficult!"

"It won't," said Snubby, beaming. "Let's bike over to Ricklesham for the day – take our lunch and everything."

"Right! That's a great idea," said Roger. "I'll go and ask Mum now. Come on, Di. Stay here, Snubby, and we'll fetch you when we're ready. So long!"

8

Off to the Fair

Mrs Lynton thought it would be a very good idea for the three to go off for a picnic. It would be a change to have a nice quiet house for once. Uncle Robert would like it too.

"Where's Snubby?" she said. "Your great-uncle has been calling all over the place for him. Has he got into trouble with him?"

"I don't think so," said Roger. "Mum, I suppose we couldn't have hard-boiled eggs, could we, and tomato sandwiches? And I suppose there aren't any jam tarts left over from yesterday, are there?"

"You're doing quite a lot of supposing," said his mother. "Suppose you go and ask Mrs Harris what she's got. She happens to be pleased with you because you took the trouble to fetch the fish for her yesterday, so I've no doubt she will look favourably on all your supposing."

Mrs Harris did. She willingly did them hard-boiled eggs, put salt and pepper into a screw of paper, made tomato and lettuce sandwiches by the dozen, added plain bread and butter for the eggs, nine jam tarts and enormous slices of ginger cake.

"Oooh I say! Can you really spare us some of that?" said Roger. "You only made it yesterday. It's chockful of bits of ginger and some chopped cherries. It's a heavenly cake."

Great-uncle appeared in the doorway. "Oh! I thought I heard you here. Have you seen Snubby?"

Roger turned to Mrs Harris. "Have you seen Snubby?" he asked innocently.

Mrs Harris shook her head. "Hasn't been near the kitchen this morning," she said. "And that's unusual. I never did see a boy that came snooping round for titbits so often. No, nor a dog either."

"It's funny I can't find him," said Great-uncle irritably. "He's always about when he's not wanted, and never here when he is. Now I've got someone coming to see me in a few minutes."

He went. Diana winked at Roger. "Did you hear that? He's got someone coming to see him – so we'll just be able to slip off nicely with Snubby. Let's get some bottles of lemonade to take with us and we'll be ready."

In five minutes' time they were ready. The lunch was packed into two neat parcels.

Roger and Diana carried the food and drink to the shed. "I'll just pop round to the study and see if Great-uncle's got his visitor yet," said Roger. He came back immediately.

"Yes, he has. Come on, get the bikes. I'll wheel Snubby's. Hurry!"

They hurried. They put the lunch into small backpacks, and strapped a big oblong box on to Snubby's back mudguard. They put a small rug inside. That was for Loony if he got tired of running beside them. He was very good at sitting in the box and going along like that.

They wheeled the bikes to the summer-house. Loony ran to meet them in delight, barking madly. Bikes meant a long, long run! No time for rabbit-holes, alas – but still a lovely long run.

Snubby peered out. He could hear them ringing their bicycle bells to tell him he was safe.

"Got everything? Oh good!" he said. "Where's Great-uncle?"

"He's seeing somebody," said Diana. "We've got the lunch and some lemonade. We've strapped on Loony's carrier too. Let's go while the going's good."

So they went. They cycled down the path and round by the window. Great-uncle Robert saw them, and stared after Snubby in exasperation.

"There he is! I thought he'd turn up just

when I couldn't see him!"

Loony ran along by Snubby's bicycle, his red tongue hanging out, feeling very happy indeed. He knew the children would not go too fast for him. If he got tired Snubby would be the first to notice and stop. Then he would be lifted into the carrier-box, and be taken along like a lord in a carriage. How Loony looked down his long black nose at the other dogs then!

"We'll picnic at the fair or near it," said Roger. "We shall have plenty of time to look at everyone then, if we're sitting down in the fair field."

"Got any money?" said Snubby, jingling his in his pocket. "I like a fair. I shall go on the roundabout and on the swings and have a go at hoopla. I threw a ring over a super torch last time."

"I've got plenty of holiday money left," said Roger. "So has Diana. More than I have. We'll be all right."

"We'll buy some ice creams too," said Diana. "You'll have to remember not to take Loony on the roundabout, Snubby. He was awfully sick last time."

"Yes. He wasted a perfectly good dinner," said Snubby. "Didn't you, Loony? Are we going too fast?"

Loony was too out of breath to answer with a bark. He didn't look tired. He loped along on his silky black legs, his long ears flap-flapping as he went.

They stopped and put him into the carrier-box after about three miles. That was as much as he could do at a run. He sat in the box panting, his tongue hanging out and looking as long as his ears!

"Now, hold tight, Loony," said Snubby, getting on again. "Here we go!"

Loony kept his balance perfectly, and enjoyed his ride enormously. Snubby didn't enjoy it quite so much because Loony was rather heavy! Still, it was better than leaving him behind.

They came to Ricklesham at last. They had a look at the house from which the valuable papers had been stolen. There was a policeman on guard at the gate. That impressed the three children very much. They got off their bicycles and looked at the big gateway.

"No one allowed in without a pass," said the policeman. "Not even a dog!"

The children grinned. "Do they know who the thief was yet?" asked Roger.

"Not a clue," said the policeman. "You on the job too?"

The children laughed and rode off. "He little knew we were on the job, more or less!" said Diana. "Now let's ask where the fair is."

They asked a woman. "Over the Longlands Field on the other side of the wood," she said, pointing.

They thanked her and rode off, Loony in the carrier again because of the traffic. They skirted the wood and came to open country. At the edge of it, in a big field, was the fair.

"Here we are!" said Roger, coming to a standstill, and leaning against the fence on his bicycle. "Looks pretty good to me. Quite a big fair."

There were round and oblong tents with flags flying. There were caravans of all colours and shapes round the field. There were horses grazing nearby, and at the far end, tied to a tree, were two enormous elephants.

The roundabout was not going. It stood there, colourful but silent, set all round with wooden animals and birds, lions, tigers, giraffes, swans, cats, dogs, bears and what looked like a chimpanzee. Swingboats were there too, but no one was using them.

"It's lunch-time, I expect," said Roger, looking at his watch. "Yes. It's a quarter to one. I expect everything will be going strong this afternoon."

"There's a shooting range over there," said Snubby. "I'll have a shot afterwards. I was pretty good last time I shot at a fair."

"Well, tell me when you're going to shoot and I'll get a mile away," said Diana. "I say, what a big fair this is – heaps of stalls and tents and things. And there's nobody that looks in the least like an anti—"

"Shut up," said Roger. "Hedges and fences have ears as much as walls. Come on – let's go through the gate and ask if we can picnic in the field. We'll say we're going to spend money at the fair afterwards."

They went through the gate, and a shock-headed boy shouted to them. "Hey, you – you're not allowed in till two o'clock."

"We're coming to the fair all afternoon," called back Roger. "We only want to have our picnic here now. Do you mind?"

"Okay," shouted the boy. He was a strange-looking fellow, with his shock of yellow hair, ears that stuck out at each side of his head, and very wide grin. He was small too, smaller than Snubby, and yet he looked about fifteen.

"Wonder what he does in the fair," said Roger, getting the lunch packet out of his backpack. "Di, you've got the drinks. Loony's biscuits are in your saddlebag, Snubby. Better keep him by us, or he'll be eaten up by that pack of mongrels over there."

Loony had no intention of wandering away if there was any lunch going. Nor did he like the look of the lean, hungry-looking dogs that were sitting down at a distance, watching. He growled at them just to tell them who he was.

It was a lovely picnic. The hard-boiled eggs went down well, and so did the sandwiches. Loony got one or two, but not many, because the children were so terribly hungry. He got no jam tart or cake, but managed to beg two pieces of bread and butter from Diana.

"What's the time? Is it two o'clock yet?" said Snubby. "I can see some people wandering along up to the gate. I expect the roundabout will start going soon."

The fair people were on the move too. Some shutters were being taken down from the stalls. A man went over to the swing-boats and idly swung one. The shock-headed boy went to the shooting range and handled a few guns, whistling shrilly.

An elephant trumpeted and made Loony jump. People came out of caravans, and hastened to various tents. The fair was opening!

The children cleared up their litter. Even Snubby was good about that. Never a scrap of paper was left lying about the grass when they had finished any picnic. Loony snuffled among the crumbs.

"Look – what's that coming along?" said Diana suddenly. "Golly – it's a monkey, isn't it. Oh, how sweet. She's coming over here to us. She's rather like Miranda, isn't she?"

The little creature came right up to them and took a flying leap to Snubby's shoulder. She whispered excitedly in his ear, and pulled his hair. The others watched intently.

"Roger – Roger, it is Miranda, I know it is!" cried Diana suddenly. And when she heard her name the tiny creature bounded up on to Diana's shoulder and put her little paw down the girl's neck – just as Miranda always used to do!

"Well, if Miranda's here, Barney is too!" cried Snubby. "Come on, let's look for him. Fancy that – Barney!"

9

Good Old Barney Again!

They passed the shooting-range, where the shock-headed boy was still polishing the guns and whistling.

"Is there a boy in the fair called Barney?" asked Roger.

"Yep. That monkey's his," said the boy, with his wide grin. "Fancy Miranda going to you like that – fussing you up good and proper, isn't she?"

"Barney *is* here!" said Diana joyfully, and the three smiled at one another. "What a bit of luck – and what a surprise too!"

Loony was jumping up, trying to reach Miranda. He knew her all right! She suddenly dropped down on his back and rode him like a horse, as she used to do. But he knew how to deal with that! He promptly rolled over and off she went. She bounded chattering on to Snubby's shoulder.

"Dear little Miranda!" said Roger, patting the tiny monkey paw. "You saw us first, didn't you – you recognised us all right and came across to us straightaway!"

"You'll find Barney up by the hoopla stall!" called the shock-headed boy. "He runs it."

They hurried to the stall he was pointing at. A boy stood there with his back to them, arranging the goods neatly on the round stall, so that people might throw hoops at them, and try to ring a prize.

"That's Barney!" cried Diana. As he heard his name the boy swung round and sure enough, it was Barney – Barney with his corn-coloured hair, his brown-as-a-berry face, his strange blue eyes set so far apart – and his wide, engaging grin.

"Well, here's a surprise!" he cried in amazement. "You kids – all three of you. Hiya, Roger, Diana! Hiya, Snubby and Loony. Still the same old mad dog, I see!"

Loony, of course, recognised Barney immediately and had hurled himself at him in his usual lunatic way, barking and whining, licking and nuzzling, doing all he could to tell Barney how pleased he was to see his friend once more.

Miranda leaped to Barney's shoulder, chattering excitedly.

"Miranda found us first," said Diana. "She came over the field to us. We didn't recognise her at first. Oh, isn't she sweet, Barney?"

"It's great to see you, great," said Barney,

his blue eyes brilliant with pleasure. "I've been thinking of you a lot – wanting to see you all again. What are you doing here? You didn't know I was here, did you?"

"No, of course not," said Roger. "We came over for a certain reason – we'll tell you about it some time when we're alone – and we never really hoped to see you, of course!"

"You might have told us you were so near us, Barney," said Diana reproachfully. "We only live a few miles away, you know."

"Is that so?" said Barney, surprised. His geography was not at all good. He never had much idea where he was, as he wandered round. "Well, how about that! I'm not much good at writing letters, anyway. Still, you're here. You on holiday or something?"

"Yes. We're home for the Easter hols," said Snubby. "We've got about three more weeks, Barney. How long are you going to be here?"

"We're here for a week," said Barney. "Excuse me for a bit – I've got to get this show going. I'm in charge of the hoopla, you know. It's not my own stall, of course. I run it for the owner. You watch Miranda and see what she does! She's a scream!"

He handed out some rings and received the money in return. The customer stood by the bar that separated her from the stall, and took aim with a wooden ring.

"Got your eye on the alarm clock, Miss?" called Barney. "Now then, steady does it!"

The ring bounced on the stall, touched the clock and lay still, half on the clock, half off. The woman tried again and yet again, using her last ring.

"Hard luck, Miss," said Barney sympathetically. "You nearly did. Miranda, get busy!"

And Miranda got busy! She leaped to the stall, gathered up the rings deftly in her tiny paws and handed them back to Barney. The children laughed in delight.

"Oh, Barney! Isn't she clever!"

"You watch her now," said Barney, as more people came up to the stall. "Go on, Miranda, do your job."

Miranda looked at him inquiringly. She made a little chattering noise and picked up a dozen or two of the wooden hoopla rings. She slipped them over her left arm. She held out her paw for the coins the people presented, and gave each one three rings!

The customers were amused and delighted. They called their children to watch Miranda, and soon there was a great crowd round the hoopla stand.

"She really is wonderful," said Diana. "Barney, you must do awfully well at this stall with Miranda to attract attention like this."

"We do," said Barney. "I've made more money at the stall than anyone else ever has. I don't get the money, of course. I give it to Tonnerre, who owns the fair, and takes it about."

"Tonnerre! What a strange name!" said Diana. "Is he French?"

"Yes, he is," said Barney, looking surprised. "How do you know?"

"Well, *tonnerre* is French for thunder," explained Diana.

"Is it really?" said Barney. "Well, I never knew he had such a good name. It suits him well!"

"Why?" asked Snubby, watching Miranda giving out rings again, and taking the money to give to Barney.

"Well, he's got a thunderous voice, and he's enormous, and he stamps about all the time," said Barney. "He's got a fearful temper, and he's an old miser – underpays everyone and kicks them out if they don't do well enough for him. There he is, over there, look – the elephants are his."

The children looked where Barney pointed. They saw the two elephants having their ropes undone from the tree, in order to take children for rides. The man with them was a giant-like fellow, with legs like tree-trunks, enormous feet, and great shoulders. He was shouting at the patient elephants, and his voice carried right over the field.

"It sounds as if somebody's turned the radio on full-blast!" said Roger with a grin. "What a voice! Tonnerre is a good name for him. He looks as black as thunder too."

"He always does," said Barney. "He's not a pleasant fellow to work with. There are about twenty people who go with the fair wherever it goes – the rest of them join it here and there, leave it, others come in their place, and so it goes on. I've been with it about four months – we've been all over the place."

"I don't like the sound of Mr Thunder," said Diana. "Is there a Mrs Lightning, by any chance?"

Barney laughed his uproarious laugh that made everyone want to laugh with him.

"No. He's not married. If anyone could be called Mrs Lightning, it's Old Ma over there – by the caravan, see? My word, her tongue's sharp as a knife. If she flashes out at anyone, they just shrivel up. Even Tonnerre goes off hurriedly if she begins to scold him!"

Ma was a peculiar-looking old woman. She looked more like a witch than anything else, as she stood stirring something in a big iron pot over the fire just outside the caravan. She had a shock of perfectly white hair, brown monkey eyes, and a chin and nose that almost met. She stood over her pot, muttering.

"I'm sure she's making a spell of some kind!" said Diana with a giggle.

"There's plenty of us show-folk that think the same," said Barney. "I don't. But lots do. They're scared stiff of Old Ma. There's only one person can do anything with her, and that's Young Un. He's the kid in charge of the shooting-range, see – over there!"

"Oh – the shock-headed boy," said Snubby. "Yes, we've seen him. He's a bit like a hobgoblin, with ears sticking right out of his head – a nice hobgoblin, though. He's got hair just like Old Ma's, only a different colour, of course – it sticks up straight like hers."

"She's his grandma," said Barney. "He gets round the old lady all right. But nobody else does. Don't you go near her – she'll fly at you like a cat!"

"Could we see the chimpanzees?" asked Diana. "We saw them advertised in a paper. They were called Hurly and Burly."

"Oh yes – they belong to Mr Vosta," said Barney. "You'll like him. Full of fun, and will do anything for you – too much sometimes. Can't say no to anyone! He's been with the fair for years, and slaves for Tonnerre day and night. I can't understand it myself. I shan't stay with this fair for long, being kicked around by that bad-tempered Tonnerre!"

The fair sounded a fascinating place, with its loud-voiced Tonnerre, its sharp-tongued Old Ma, the shock-headed Young Un, Vosta and his chimpanzees – and Barney and Miranda, of course. The three children stood by the hoopla stall and looked round the fair eagerly, wondering which of all these people would be the most likely to be the thief who could get through locked doors and fastened windows.

They hadn't told Barney about that yet.

There hadn't been a chance, with customers coming and going. It would be best not to say anything till they were quite alone with him.

"You go on round the fair and have a look-see for yourselves," said Barney. "I could leave Miranda here to look after the stall – she's as good at it as I am – but if Tonnerre sees I'm gone he'll yell the place down."

"Right, we'll come back later. My word, it *was* a surprise to see you, Barney! Best surprise we've had these hols!"

10

An Interesting Afternoon

They went round the fair, looking at everything and trying everything too. They went on the roundabouts and on the swings, they rode on the elephants and they paid to go in and see the wonderful chimpanzees. They didn't miss a thing!

"Make the roundabout go as fast as you can," Snubby said to the boy in charge of it.

"Hold on tight then," said the boy, with a grin. "What about your dog?"

"No. He's sick if he goes on," said Snubby. "He'll sit by you and wait. Sit, Loony, sit!"

He chose the chimpanzees, and the others chose the lions. The wooden animals went up and down as well as round and round. The music began to play, and the roundabout moved off.

The boy kept his word and ran the machinery as fast as it would go. The children had to cling tightly to the animals or they would have been thrown off. Diana began to feel sick. The other three riders began to yell at the boy.

He slowed it down and grinned again. "That all right for you?" he asked Snubby, who was now looking slightly green, and found that he couldn't walk straight. Nor could the others.

"It was wizard," said Snubby. "Faster than I've ever been. It was worth the double fare!"

Not only the roundabout had gone fast, but the music too – and Tonnerre had heard it, of course. His face went purple, and he yelled at the roundabout boy. But the music was so loud that the boy didn't hear the yells. It was only when the roundabout had stopped and Tonnerre had parked his elephants for a minute, shouting all the while, that the poor boy knew what he was in for!

"You! You, boy! You toad of a boy!" yelled Mr Tonnerre in his thunderous voice. "What you think you do, eh? You want to make people sick? You want to break my machine? Ar-rr-r-r-r-r-r!"

He finished off with a noise so like the growl of a giant dog that Loony was astonished, and leaped to his feet. *Biff!* Tonnerre gave the roundabout boy a clip round the ear. Snubby stepped forward.

"Mr Tonnerre! It was my fault. I paid him double fare to go fast."

It looked as if Mr Tonnerre was about to box his ears too. Then he turned to the roundabout boy, "Ah! Aha! Double fare. Where is the money? You think to keep it for yourself! Give me all the money you have got. Queek, queek!"

"Queek, queek!" apparently meant "Quick, quick." Mr Tonnerre had a most peculiar accent, English and French mixed up with American and Cockney. He towered over everyone, as elephantine as his two elephants.

He turned to Snubby next. "You come to ride on my elephants, no, yes? For double fare I make them trit-trot like horses. Yes!"

"No thanks," said Snubby. "I mean – yes, I'd like to ride on your elephants, but no trit-trotting, thank you. I don't feel as if I could bear a trotting elephant."

So they rode on the great elephants, and swayed from side to side in a most alarming manner. Loony refused to get up with Snubby. He retired behind a tree, very much afraid of the enormous creatures that appeared to have tails in front as well as behind.

"Now you go watch Mr Billy Tell," said Mr Tonnerre in his enormous voice, as he helped them off the elephants. "He very, very clever man. Crick-crack, his gun goes, and off goes the apple on Young Un's head."

"Billy Tell does the same act as William Tell, who was probably his great-great-great-great-great-uncle," remarked Roger, as they made their way to a tent marked in enormous red letters BILLY TELL.

Old Ma shambled over to look after the shooting-range when Young Un went to stand inside Billy Tell's tent with an apple perched high on his shock of hair. He grinned as the children came in to watch.

"Hiya!" he said. "Come to watch my hair being singed?"

Billy Tell was dressed in a cowboy suit, and looked rather grand. He would have looked grander if he hadn't been quite so dirty. There was a long wait until enough people had paid to come into the tent.

Billy Tell sat looking bored, with his gun across his knee. Young Un cleverly walked about, round the tent, balancing the apple on his head all the time and collecting the entrance money.

The news had got round that it was Snubby who had paid double fare to the roundabout boy to make the roundabout go fast. Young Un came up to him, grinning.

"Sure you haven't paid double to see Billy shoot off the tips of my ears?" he asked Snubby.

Snubby liked him. "You bet I have," he said. "So look out!"

He hadn't, of course, and Young Un knew

it. He stood with his back to a steel sheet, the apple on his head. Billy Tell stood up at last and walked to the other end of the tent.

He took aim casually. *BANG!* The apple was split into a hundred bits and pieces, and Young Un wiped some out of his eyes.

He set another on his head. Billy Tell put his head between his legs and took aim from there. *BANG!* Again the apple split into tiny pieces. Everyone applauded loudly. Loony crouched against Snubby's legs, frightened at the bangs so near to him.

Young Un wiped his face again and walked over to the children. "Good shooting!" he said. "I'm a good shot too – a jolly good one. I shot a weathercock off a steeple once."

"Garn!" said Billy Tell's drawling voice. "You and your tales! Here, take my gun and clean it. And tell Old Ma I'll have sausages for my supper tonight."

"Yes, Dad," said Young Un, and somehow the children felt surprised. So Billy Tell was his father and Old Ma was his grandmother. What an interesting family to have!

"Have you got a mother?" asked Snubby.

"Naw! One woman in the family is enough for me to manage!" said Young Un, winking towards Old Ma as she stood at her shooting-range.

"Say, Ma," he said to her as they came up. "Billy Tell says please to give him sausages tonight."

"Sausages!" squealed the old lady. "What does he think I am? Sausages cost money, you tell him, the varmint, and rabbits and hares don't cost nothing at all if they're shot – and what's his gun for, I'd like to know? Think he's got it just for shooting apples off your turnip head! Where is he? I'll give him sausages, so I will!"

"Well, Ma, that's all he asked you to give him – sausages!" yelled Young Un cheekily, and put his hands behind his sticking-out ears the better to hear all the rude names Old Ma called him as she went back to her caravan.

Snubby had a turn with a gun, trying his hardest to shoot one of the ping-pong balls that bobbed up and down on the top of the little fountain of water spouting continually at the back of the range. But he couldn't shoot one.

Young Un took a quick glance to see if Billy Tell, Old Ma or Tonnerre were anywhere near. Then he took a gun, aimed it – and *bang* went one ping-pong ball, *bang* went another, *bang* went a third! There was no doubt about it, Young Un was a very good shot. Snubby quite believed he had once shot a weathercock down!

"Now you choose a prize," he said to Snubby. "Go on – I like you. Choose one of these here prizes."

"But I didn't shoot the balls off the water," said Snubby in astonishment.

"Don't matter, I did, and nobody's to know that," said Young Un. "I like you, see – no stuck-up nonsense about you or your dog. Go on, quick – take a prize. What about them there toffees. They're good."

It took Snubby quite a long time to convince Young Un that he thought it wrong to take a prize he hadn't won. Young Un gave way at last, but he didn't understand in the least. He didn't seem to know what honesty meant where that kind of thing was concerned.

"It's awfully nice of you," poor Snubby kept saying, "but it isn't right."

"Aw shucks," said Young Un, and gave in. "You better go with the others now. They're yelling to you to have a swing. Choose the boat at the end. It's best and you can make it go high."

What with roundabout riding, elephant riding, shooting, going in swing-boats, and sampling all kinds of other things, the children hadn't much money left by the end of the day! They had bought themselves enormous sticky buns in the snack-tent, and slices of cake, and lemonade, and had carried a good share over to Barney, who was still in charge of the hoopla, and doing very well; partly, of course, because of Miranda's amusing antics.

"When do you get off?" asked Diana. "We shall have to be going soon. Couldn't you come back to supper with us?"

"I'd like to do that," said Barney, his eyes shining with delight at the invitation. "I'll get Young Un to take over from me. Old Ma always takes over from him about now. If I pay him, he'll come to my stall. I'm due for an evening off, so Tonnerre can't say anything if I go. Sure your mother won't mind me coming?"

"She won't mind; she wants to meet

95

you," said Roger. "We've told her all about you – how we met you last summer and had that adventure at Rockingdown. How can you get to our place? We biked."

"Oh, I can borrow a bike," said Barney. "Miranda can either ride on my shoulder or on the handlebars, she doesn't mind which."

"She can ride in the carrier-box with Loony if she likes!" said Snubby. But she didn't like. She preferred to ride in the middle of Barney's handlebars, her soft monkey-hair streaming backwards in the wind.

They left the fair behind. It was noisy and crowded now. The stall-keepers were shouting, people were laughing, the roundabout was playing its harsh music. Snubby wished he could stay.

"Come on," said Roger, as he lingered behind. "We'll be late. And don't forget we've got to tell Barney our secret – we'll have to make time for that!"

Yes – their secret. Barney might be able to help them over that. How surprised he would be when they told him!

11

Barney Comes to Supper

"I shall have to be careful not to give Great-uncle a chance to nab me and ask me awkward questions," said Snubby as they rode off.

"It will be easy to get out of that if we've got a guest with us," said Roger. "Look where you're going, Snubby, you idiot – you rode over that hole and nearly tipped poor Loony out of his box."

"Sorry, Loony!" called back Snubby.

Barney had tried to clean himself up a little in order to meet Mrs Lynton. He put on clean flannel trousers, and a clean, or nearly clean, sweater; his shoes were bad but he could do nothing about those because he had on his one and only pair! His toe was beginning to poke out of one, and Roger wondered if he had a pair that would fit Barney; but it looked as if Barney's feet were bigger than his.

They arrived home tired and hungry. Loony leaped thankfully out of the carrier and ran straight to the kitchen to beg for a bone. Mrs Harris wasn't there. But there was a dish of sardines put down for the cat. Loony went over and sniffed at it. Should he take a bit? He was so hungry. No – it smelled nasty. Let Sardine the cat have it!

Sardine came in and spat at him. He ran at her and she fled out of the kitchen, along the passage and up the stairs. Into Roger's room she went, and leaped up on the chest of drawers.

Somebody else was sitting there! It was Miranda the monkey, waiting for the boys. Sardine got the shock of her life. She had never seen a monkey before.

She went off like a firework, fizzing and hissing and spitting, her tail three times its size. Miranda looked at her in horror. Whatever was this explosive animal?

In a fright, Miranda leaped down to the floor, scampered on all fours across the room, out on to the landing, and into Great-uncle Robert's room. He was there, brushing his mane of silver hair. He was startled to see a monkey leap on to his bed. Then came Sardine, and after Sardine came an excited Loony. The three of them rushed round the room twice and then disappeared.

Great-uncle sat down suddenly. What a household! A monkey! Had he seen right? Really, his bedroom was becoming a menagerie. He would have to speak to

Susan about it. No guest could be expected to put up with hordes of monkeys, cats, and dogs running in circles round his bedroom.

Roger was trying out his shoes on Barney. They were too small. Roger remembered what a lot of shoes Great-uncle had. Surely he could spare a pair. He went along and knocked at the door.

"Who is it now?" asked Great-uncle Robert pettishly, as if he half-expected some more animals.

"It's me, Roger," said Roger. "Great-uncle, have you an old pair of shoes you could give me?"

"What's come over this household?" said Great-uncle. "First my bedroom's full of . . . oh, well, never mind. What on earth do you want a pair of my shoes for? They won't fit you!"

"It's for a friend of mine who's come to supper," explained Roger.

"Did he come without shoes then?" asked Great-uncle. "Good heavens, there's that monkey again! If I can find out who's brought a monkey to this house and let it loose, I'll . . . I'll . . . I'll . . ."

Roger departed hurriedly. If Great-uncle knew it was the owner of the monkey who wanted the shoes he wouldn't lend them or give them, that was certain. "Come on, Miranda, you little wretch!" he said to the excited monkey. "Don't rush all over the place. You'll give my mother a fit if she meets you on the stairs."

He rummaged in the hall cupboard and found an old pair of tennis shoes belonging to his father. At least Barney's toes wouldn't stick out of those. Barney put them on gratefully.

"Do I look too awful to come to supper with you?" he asked Diana anxiously, when she came to see if the boys were ready.

"No, you're quite all right," she said, hoping that her mother would think so too – and even more, her father. "I've told Mummy you're here. She *is* looking forward to meeting you."

Barney was nervous. He had seldom been in a big house, and he was afraid his manners were bad. But he needn't have worried. He had naturally good manners, and a pleasant voice. When Mrs Lynton saw his strange blue eyes, set so wide, and noticed the anxious expression in them, she gave him an even warmer welcome than she had planned.

"So you're Barney! I've heard all about you. Richard, this is Barney, the boy who went through those hair-raising adventures with our three last summer."

Mr Lynton looked up. He expected to see a foreign-looking boy, sly and shrewd. Instead he saw Barney, with his bright, corn-coloured hair brushed back, his honest eyes, and straight, fearless look. He held out his hand.

"You're welcome, Barney," he said. "Any friend of Roger's is a friend of mine."

Roger's heart warmed to his father. Good old Dad! He might be hot-tempered and strict and all the rest of it – but he had the right thoughts and feelings every time. Barney blushed with relief and pleasure. What nice parents Roger and Diana had – and how lucky they were!

"Mummy – do you mind Miranda?" asked Diana anxiously, as she saw her mother's eyes stray in the monkey's direction for the first time. Miranda was sitting demurely on the back of a chair.

"Oh dear!" said her mother, and began to laugh helplessly. "Richard – do look at that. I don't think I shall mind her, Diana, if she doesn't come too near me. I really don't like monkeys, you know."

"Shall I take her out?" asked Barney at once.

"No, no," said Mrs Lynton. "If I can put up willingly with Sardine and Loony, I can surely put up with a harmless little creature like this. But what your great-uncle will say I cannot imagine."

Great-uncle was a little late for the meal. Loony had hidden his evening shoes and it took him a long time to find them. When he came down at last, it was to find the family very friendly indeed with Barney and Miranda. It would have been difficult for him to make any trouble about them.

Barney thoroughly enjoyed himself. He loved the well-cooked food, the chatter, the laughter, the spotless mats, the flowers on the table, in fact, everything. Mrs Lynton liked him very much. How could this boy be a circus boy, a boy who wandered about with fairs, who probably hardly ever had a bath – and yet was nice enough to make a good friend for her son?

Mr Lynton liked Barney too. "Have you no parents?" he asked.

"My mother died some time ago," answered Barney. "I never knew my father. He doesn't know anything about me, I'm afraid. All I know is that he's an actor, Mr Lynton – and used to act in Shakespeare's plays. I've been looking for him all over the place, but I haven't found him yet."

"Do you know his stage-name?" asked Mr Lynton, thinking that surely any father would like to have a son like this turning up to claim him.

Barney shook his head. "No, I don't even know what he looks like. I don't know his right name either, Mr Lynton, because my mother was in the circus, and took *her* name always, not her married name. I'm afraid I'll never find him."

"It seems doubtful, I must say," said Mr

Lynton. "Well, – you seem to have done quite well on your own."

After supper the four children went out into the garden. It was about half past eight, and still light. They went into the summer-house and put Loony on guard again.

Miranda came too, of course. She had been on her very best behaviour at supper-time, and sat on Barney's shoulder all the time, accepting pieces of tomato from him, and a few apricot slices from the pudding dish. Now she sat on Snubby's shoulder, and tucked her little paws into his collar to keep them warm. He loved her. Loony was jealous and tried to get up on Snubby's knee.

"Now – what is it you wanted to tell me?" Barney asked, when Loony had been sent outside on guard.

"Well," said Roger, hardly knowing how to begin. "It's a peculiar story really – our great-uncle is mixed up in it too. It's like this . . ."

He told the whole tale, with the others joining in occasionally.

"So you see," he ended, "we did just wonder if the fair has got anything to do with the robberies – whether somebody in the fair knows enough about old papers and documents to steal them when the show goes near a museum, or near any other place where it's known that valuable papers are kept."

"And we want to find out how the thief can go through locked doors," said Diana. "It's a bit like magic. You'd want a spell to do that!"

"Perhaps it's Old Ma!" said Snubby, remembering how witch-like she looked, bent over her iron pot.

Everyone laughed. Barney sat in silence, considering. "I don't know anyone in the fair who's interested in old things except Tonnerre," he said at last. "Tonnerre collects tiny carved ivory statues – but I've never heard of him collecting old papers. I shouldn't have thought he was educated enough to know whether they were valuable or not – or even where to go for them."

"And surely he couldn't go through locked doors!" said Diana, remembering how enormous Tonnerre was.

"No, he couldn't," said Barney.

There was a silence. "Who decides the place where the fair is to go?" asked Diana suddenly.

"Well – Tonnerre, I suppose, as he owns the fair," said Barney. "Why? Oh – I see what you mean. Somebody knows where rare papers can be got – and that somebody decides to take the fair there, in order to steal them. Yes – well, as far as I know Tonnerre always decides. He gives the orders, anyway."

"Does anyone else in the fair collect

anything?" asked Snubby, playing with Miranda's tail.

"No – only Burly, one of the chimps!" said Barney with a laugh. "He collects toy animals – didn't you know? If you'll only give him a toy animal he'll be your slave for life! Odd, isn't it?"

"Very odd," said Diana, and laughed. "What does Hurly collect?"

"Sweets! But they don't last long!" said Barney. "You have to be careful of your pockets with Hurly. If you've got any sweets or chocolates there he'll pick your pockets as quickly as anything."

"We really must make friends with them," said Diana. "We hardly spoke to them today, there was so many things to see. Well, Barney, you can't really help us much, can you, about the probable thief in the fair – except that it is more likely to be Tonnerre than anyone else."

"There's Vosta," said Barney thoughtfully. "And there's Billy Tell. Both artful as can be. But somehow I can't see either of them knowing about rare papers. Why, I don't believe Billy Tell can read!"

"Oh well – perhaps it really is just chance that the burglaries occur when the fair is in the district," said Diana. "I wonder where it's going to next."

"Didn't I tell you? It's coming near here," said Barney. "About a mile away, I think.

On Dolling Hill over at Rilloby."

"How smashing!" said Snubby. "How absolutely super. We'll see you every single day then – and I'll tell you what – we'll take it in turns to watch old Tonnerre! I *bet* he's the one. I've a feeling in my bones!"

12

Plans!

The four children talked for a long while that night in the summerhouse. Now that Barney, too, seemed to think that Diana's "hunch" might have something in it, they were keener than ever to solve the mystery.

Snubby had an unexpectedly good idea. "I say, I wonder if there's any place at Rilloby or near there that has a museum or rare collections of any kind," he said.

"Now that's a brainwave of yours," said Diana warmly. "You don't often have a brainwave – but that really is an idea."

"Yes. If we find out any place like that near the fair, or within a mile or two, we could perhaps watch it," suggested Roger.

"Yes – watch it and see if Tonnerre came snooping about," said Snubby.

"We couldn't help seeing him if he did, he's so enormous!" said Diana.

"And if we did see him wandering about we could go to the place at night and see if we could catch him getting in," went on

Snubby excitedly. "We might learn a thing or two about locked doors and how to get through them then!"

Everyone began suddenly to feel very excited. Could they really do all this? Well, perhaps they couldn't – but it would be very exciting to try.

"The thing to do first is to find out whether there is a museum or anything near Rilloby," said Roger.

"How can we do that?" asked Diana. "I've never heard of one – and we've lived here for years."

"It might not be a museum," said Roger. "It might be a private collection of some sort – like the one Great-uncle was arranging at Chelie Manor House. Gosh, I know how to find out!"

"How?" said everyone.

"Well, ask Great-uncle, of course!" said Roger triumphantly. "He'd know. I do believe he knows werc every single valuable letter, map, plan, chronicle and all the rest of it is in the whole of Great Britain. He really is very learned, you know. These anti-quarians are."

"Anti what?" inquired Barney, who had never heard the word before. Diana explained.

Barney listened solemnly. He always liked to pick up any bit of knowledge that he could.

"Well, now – who's to ask Great-uncle about this?" said Roger.

"Not me," said Snubby promptly. "He'd think I was getting the information out of him to hand to the Green Hands Gang!"

"Don't be an idiot," said Diana.

"He would," said Snubby firmly. "He may be learned and all the rest of it, but he believes anything you tell him. I mean, he swallowed all about the Green Hands Gang and the rest of it absolutely whole! You should have seen his hair stand on end when I told him."

"Don't exaggerate," said Roger. "Anyway, we wouldn't dream of you asking him anything. You'd only make a mess of it, and say something silly."

Snubby subsided. Diana considered the question. "I'll ask him," she said. "I'll take my autograph book to him for his autograph – he'll like that – and then I'll get him talking about collections of signatures or something like that and from that I'll get to other collections of papers – and I can ask him what I want to know quite casually. He won't suspect a thing."

"That's well worked out, Di," said Roger approvingly. "You do that tomorrow. Snubby had better still keep out of Great-uncle's way, in case he's asking too many awkward questions about how he knew there was to be a robbery at Ricklesham.

You really were an idiot over that, Snubby."

"All right, all right, tell me again," said Snubby sulkily. "Always going on at me – and yet I thought of the best idea this evening."

"Yes, it was a good idea," said Roger. "We'll let it cancel out that mistake of yours! I say, isn't it getting dark!"

"Mummy will be after us in a minute, saying it's bedtime," said Diana.

"Then I'd better go," said Barney, and he got up. "This has been a lovely evening for me. Thanks an awful lot. Are you coming to the fair tomorrow?"

"Of course," said Diana. "We'll see you every day till we go back to school, Barney. I'm glad Mummy likes you. You can come here often now."

"Dad likes him too," said Roger. "Well, see you tomorrow, Barney. Is Miranda asleep? She's been awfully quiet."

"Sound asleep," said Barney. "She's inside my shirt. Feel her – warm as toast. She works hard at the hoopla stall with me, you know. Loony's been quiet too. I suppose he's tired out with his long run."

He was! He was stretched out on the step of the summerhouse sound asleep too.

"He hasn't been much good as a watch-dog this evening!" said Roger, poking him with his foot. "Wake up, you sleepy hound! Didn't you know you were on guard?"

"Woof," said Loony and sat up suddenly.

"Goodbye, Barney," said Diana. "I'm awfully glad we've found you again. Don't forget to keep an eye on Tonnerre."

"I'll remember," said Barney with a laugh. "His caravan stands near to ours. I'll keep an ear open all night now to hear if he creeps out of his van – and I'll watch to see if he puts his light on in the middle of the night."

"And if he creeps out, follow him," said Roger.

Barney slipped away to his bicycle. Mrs Lynton's voice could be heard calling the children. It was quite dark now, but the evening was very warm for April.

"I like the smell of those wallflowers," said Snubby, sniffing hard as they walked down the path. "Now, if I were a dog I'd go round sniffing at all the nice-smelling flowers – they'd just be the right height for sniffing."

"Look – there's Great-uncle standing by Mummy," said Diana, clutching Snubby. "I bet he's waiting to have a few quiet words with you, Snubby."

"Gosh," said Snubby, and stopped.

"Go to bed quickly," said Roger. "Go in the back way and slip up the stairs. Don't undress. Get into bed at once, so that if Great-uncle comes up to find you, you'll look fast asleep. Quick!"

Snubby slipped round to the back door, ran through the kitchen, and disappeared upstairs, Loony at his heels. He fell over Sardine on the way, of course, and Loony took the opportunity of getting in a little nip as he passed. Aha! That would teach Sardine to lie in wait on the stairs. An explosive spitting noise followed Loony as he bounded off.

Snubby ran into his bedroom, slipped off his shoes without unlacing them, and flung himself under the sheets. He left out just the top of his shock of red hair.

"Where's Snubby?" said Mrs Lynton, when the others appeared at the door. "Great-uncle wants a word with him."

"Oh, dear. I think he's gone to bed," said Diana.

"Has he?" said her mother, astonished to hear that he had gone to bed before he was sent. It was usually quite a job to get Snubby off to bed. "He must be very tired."

"Well, we went on a long bike-ride today," said Roger. "I'll say goodnight too, Mum. I'm half asleep already. Did you like Barney?"

"Very much," said his mother. "Ask him here whenever you like. And – if you can tell him without offending him – say to him that he can have a hot bath whenever he'd like one. I'm sure there are never any hot baths at a fair."

"Oh, Mum – you would think of that!" said Roger with a laugh. He gave her a hug. "I'm so glad you liked him. Goodnight and sweet dreams. Goodnight, Great-uncle."

"Goodnight," said Great-uncle. "Er – I'll just come up with you and see if Snubby's asleep. I really do want a word with him."

He went up with them. Mrs Lynton went too, rather puzzled. Why did Uncle Robert keep wanting to talk to Snubby? What could Snubby have done?

Nothing was to be seen of Snubby but a tuft of red hair, and a small mound under the bedclothes. Loony was lying on his feet.

"Fast asleep!" said Mrs Lynton. "Don't disturb him, Uncle Robert. He's tired out. Oh dear – look at Loony on the bed. I

don't like to take him off in case I wake Snubby."

Snubby gave a gentle little snore. "Idiot!" thought Roger. "Now he's going to overdo things as usual."

"Well – I'll talk to him tomorrow," said Great-uncle, and he and Mrs Lynton went out.

"Snubby, they've gone," said Roger and pulled the clothes down. But Snubby didn't move. He was fast asleep! In all his clothes too.

"What a boy!" said Diana. "Let him be. He's *really* tired out. So's Loony – not a flicker in him! Goodnight, Roger. We'll have some fun now we've found old Barney again!"

13

Diana Does Her Bit

Most fortunately for Snubby, Great-uncle Robert had one of his bad nights that night, and asked to have his breakfast in bed the next day.

Snubby was full of glee. "I thought I'd have to get down early to breakfast, gulp a bit of porridge and make that do," he said, "so as to be away from the table when Great-uncle came down. But now I shall be able to have a proper breakfast. Good-oh!"

"We'll go over to the fair after lunch today," said Diana. "I've got to help Mum do all the flowers and turn out some of my cupboards. We could take tea over to Ricklesham and have it with Barney. We'll take enough for him too."

"And that will give you a chance to get on to Great-uncle about any museum or private collection," said Roger. "Snubby, you'd better spend the morning doing errands for Mrs Harris. Then you'll be out of the way."

"Oh," said Snubby, who was never very

116

keen on doing errands. "All right. I'll see if Mrs Harris wants anything. She said something about somebody fetching a new doormat for the back door. I'd have to go to Rilloby for that."

"Well, that would take you out of Great-uncle's way for ages," said Diana. "You can go mooching round the toyshops, and have a few ice creams, and forget where you've left your bike, and take ages finding it again and—"

"Don't try and be funny, Diana," said Snubby, giving her a push. "You'll be an old nagger when you grow up if you don't look out. Like Old Ma!"

"I shan't – and don't push me like that," said Diana, shoving back. "Why do little boys give people pushes and shoves when they get annoyed?"

"Same reason as big girls do, I expect," said Snubby, and went off pleased with himself.

He went to the kitchen and asked Mrs Harris if there were any errands she wanted done. She stared at him in surprise.

"What's come over you? Want me to make you meringues or something for lunch?"

"Oh no – I mean yes – well, no, I don't ask you for that reason," said Snubby, getting into a muddle. "What I mean is, meringues didn't enter my head – but if they're in yours and you want to make them for lunch, well, all I can say is, you go ahead!"

"You're after something, I know!" said Mrs Harris. "Well, I'll think about the meringues. And seeing you are suddenly so helpful, yes, I'd be glad if you could get the new doormat for the back door. I keep on and on about it but nobody fetches it."

"I'll fetch it, Mrs Harris," said Snubby. "Anything else?"

"Well, bless me, you can't be feeling yourself to come and ask for jobs," said Mrs Harris. "Still, I may as well take advantage of it! You can bring back the kippers with you – and seeing that you're going all the way to Rilloby, would you call at the cobbler's and collect my best shoes, and . . ."

"Here! Wait a minute! I haven't got all day to spare," said Snubby, suddenly feeling that he was taking on more than he had bargained for.

"I was just about to finish and say I'd be making meringues for your lunch," said Mrs Harris with a twinkle.

"You'd better write all those things down while I get my bike," said Snubby. "I'll be back in half a jiffy."

He came back and took the list from Mrs Harris. She had added one or two other things to it. It was a real chance to get everything brought back, with Snubby in such a rare and unusually obliging mood!

"I'll just give you a jam tart to munch before you go," said Mrs Harris, and went to the cupboard. "Oh, by the way, your Great-uncle was in here a minute ago asking for you."

Snubby vanished at once, without even waiting for the jam tart. Mrs Harris was most surprised.

Great-uncle marched into the lounge, where Mrs Lynton was doing the flowers. "I'm looking for Snubby," he said.

Mrs Lynton leaned out of the window and called to Diana, who was picking daffodils for the vases. "Diana! Where's Snubby? Great-uncle wants him."

"Oh, Mum – he's just gone to Rilloby on his bike," said Diana, coming to the window. "He told me he's fetching the new doormat for the back door, and he's bringing back the kippers, and fetching some mended shoes, and . . ."

Mrs Lynton couldn't believe her ears. "Snubby is doing all that – on his own?" she asked disbelievingly. "What's come over him?"

"Oh, he can be helpful when he likes," said Diana, and turned away to hide a smile. "I'm afraid he won't be back for ages, Great-uncle."

"A nuisance this," grumbled Great-uncle Robert, crossly. "Slippery as an eel, that boy. Anyone would think he was avoiding me."

"Oh, no, Uncle Robert," said Mrs Lynton. "Of course he's not. Why should he?"

"I shan't be in to lunch, my dear," said Great-uncle, not bothering to answer her. "I'm going up to London to see an old friend of mine."

"Oh, Great-uncle – before you go will you sign my autograph album?" called Diana suddenly. Dear me, she mustn't let him slip off without asking him a few important questions!

"Ask your Great-uncle another time, dear," said her mother exasperatingly. "He's off to catch a train."

"Oh, I'm not going just yet," said Great-uncle, beaming at Diana. "I'll sign Diana's album. I've got a sixteenth-century proverb I once found in an old document that I'll write in for her – and I'll write it exactly as I saw it, in the old printing."

"Oh, thank you," said Diana. "I'll get my album now. I'll bring it into the study, Great-uncle. I expect you'll be in there."

"I will, my dear, I will," said Great-uncle. So Diana took her album there, and the old man painstakingly printed in old letters the sixteenth-century proverb he had once found.

"There!" he said. "Can you read that?"

"When ye thunder-clouds come, think on the storm-cock bird – he sings," Diana read with difficulty, for the shape of the letters and the spelling of the words were strange.

"Very nice, isn't it," said Great-uncle. "We haven't a saying like that in these modern times."

"Well, we have, really," said Diana. "You know: When you're up to your neck in hot water, think of the kettle – and sing!'"

"Ah – h'm!" said Great-uncle, surprised. "I've not heard that. Typical of these times – flippant, my dear, flippant, where the other proverb is beautiful."

Diana wasn't sure what flippant meant. It somehow reminded her of tiddly-winks. Yes, you flipped the counters – so they were probably flippant. She decided not to enter into that question, but to push on with what she wanted to know.

"Great-uncle, you know an awful lot about old things, don't you?" she said.

"Yes, my dear. It's always been my great interest – delving into the past, spreading my net there, and seeing what I can bring up," said Great-uncle.

"You've brought up some wonderful old things, haven't you?" said Diana.

"Well, you probably wouldn't think they were wonderful," said Great-uncle. "I'm interested really in old writings, you know – particularly old letters, which give us a vivid picture of the times in which they were written."

"I suppose you know every collection in the country?" said Diana in an awed voice.

Great-uncle was flattered at Diana's interest. "No, no," he said. "I know the most famous ones, of course – and many of the minor ones – but not all, my dear, no, not all!"

"Are there any interesting collections near here, Great-uncle?" asked Diana, bringing out her important question quite airily. She was pleased with herself! "Any near Rilloby, for instance?"

"Now let me see," said Great-uncle, considering. "Well, there's Marloes Castle, of course, but there's only a very small collection there. Lord Marloes was more interested in animals and birds than old documents. He's got a fine collection of those, so I hear – began to stuff them himself as a boy."

"Are the documents valuable – very valuable?" asked Diana.

"Yes – yes, I suppose they are," said Great-uncle. "I know some Americans were after them last year, so Marloes told me. He wouldn't sell, though. They're all family letters and historical documents relating to his own estate – he'd never part with them. He wouldn't part with his stuffed animals either! Now – I wonder – I believe I can get in touch with him in town. Would you and the others like to go and see his collection of animals, if I can get you permission?"

"Oh, yes please, Great-uncle," said Diana, delighted. This was a bit of luck. They could have a good look round the collections, and see the lie of the land – then if there happened to be a burglary there they would be able to picture the rooms and everything.

"Well, I'll telephone Marloes and see if he's back in town," said Great-uncle. "I'll take you over to the old castle myself, and you can look at the stuffed animals and I'll have another look at the documents. It'll be quite a day out, won't it, my dear?"

"Oh, yes," said Diana. "Thanks awfully, Great-uncle. We'd all love to come."

"Dear, dear, look at the time!" said Great-uncle, getting up in a hurry. "I shall miss that train."

He went off, and Diana closed her album thoughtfully. She considered she had done very well indeed. She had found out where valuable papers were – in Marloes Castle – and it was possible that Great-uncle would take her and the others there – and they would be able to do a good snoop round. Wonderful!

She went out to find Roger. "Roger! Roger! Where are you? Quick, I've got good news."

Mrs Lynton heard her calling, and saw her talking excitedly to Roger. What could the "good news" be, she wondered. How surprised she would have been if she had known!

14

At the Fair Again

Snubby arrived home complete with everything Mrs Harris had asked for. She beamed at him. "There are two meringues for each of you," she told him, "and there's one over. I'll tell your aunt I made it specially for you. So you can have three."

"Smashing!" said Snubby, pleased. "I say, this doormat thing was frightfully awkward. I shall think twice before I say I'll fetch one again."

"Oh, we shan't want one for years," said Mrs Harris. "Loony, come out of the larder. Bless us all, if I leave that larder door open for so much as half a moment that dog's in there."

"Loony!" yelled Snubby, and Loony backed out hurriedly. Oh, the smells in a larder! It was a far, far better place than the biggest, smelliest rabbit-hole.

Roger and Diana went to tell Snubby the news about Marloes Castle. He was excited.

"That's a bit of luck. You're clever, Di, to

manage all that. How did you wangle it?"

"Easy," said Diana. "Great-uncle lapped up all I said."

"I told you he'd swallow anything," said Snubby. "Now you can see why he swallowed my Green Hands Gang yarn."

"Well, if he really does get permission to take us over the collection, and there's a burglary some time, we'll be able to picture how it's done," said Roger. "We'll make a plan of the rooms where the collections are – or anyway of the room where the papers are. The thief won't be interested in the stuffed animals."

They had a very good lunch indeed, and enjoyed Mrs Harris's meringues immensely. They wished there were far, far more.

"Can't you go shopping for Mrs Harris every single morning?" said Diana to Snubby.

"No, I can't," said Snubby decidedly. "If you want meringues again, you go shopping for her. I've done my bit. My bike almost broke down with all the weight it had to carry. Poor Loony had to run all the way back. I couldn't possibly carry him as well. Anyway, the carrier-box was full of shoes and things."

"Are you going to see Barney today?" said Mrs Lynton after lunch. "If so, take him this shirt, will you? It's one that's too small for your father, and it would do for him nicely. It should be the right size."

"Right, Mum. He'll be pleased," said Roger. "We're just off now. Mrs Harris has packed us up some tea. It'll be nice for you to have an afternoon without us or Great-uncle, won't it!"

They were off at last, and Mrs Lynton sank down thankfully on the sofa with a book. Now for peace!

They arrived at the fair after it had opened and heard the roundabout music a long way away. Barney was on the lookout for them. He waved cheerily as they came up. Young Un waved too, and so did the roundabout boy. Now that it was known that they were Barney's friends they were welcome any time, whether they had money to spend or not.

There was no one at the hoopla stall just then. Hurly and Burly, the two chimpanzees, were giving their show in Vosta's tent and most people had gone to see them.

They were able to tell Barney their news about Marloes Castle.

"Jolly good," grinned Barney. "I've got no news, I'm afraid. I've kept an eye on Tonnerre, but he's done nothing suspicious. All I've heard is that we move to Rilloby tomorrow."

"I saw the notices this morning," said Snubby. "There were posters advertising Rilloby Fair all over the place."

"It'll be easier for you to see me when we're there," said Barney. "Nearer for you."

"Where's Miranda?" asked Snubby, missing the little monkey suddenly.

"Gone to watch Hurly and Burly do their tricks," said Barney. "They love her, you know. Hold her and nurse her like a baby – especially Burly, the one that likes the toy animals."

"Could we go and peep in at Hurly and Burly?" asked Diana. "Have they finished yet?"

"Almost," said Barney. "I'll take you over. There's nobody likely to come to the hoopla stall till the chimps' show is over. Look out for Old Ma today. She's in one of her tempers. Even Tonnerre is keeping away from her."

They kept an eye open for Old Ma, but they didn't see her. They heard her though, muttering loudly in her caravan. Young Un saw them as they went by and winked.

"Have to go and give Old Ma a spanking soon," he said with a grin. "Getting above herself, she is!"

Barney took them to Vosta's tent. He nodded to the attendant and let them peep inside. Hurly and Burly were just finishing their performance. Burly was riding a bicycle made specially for him, and Hurly was standing on the handlebars, turning somersaults as the bicycle went round and round

the small ring of grass. He landed neatly
back on the handlebars each time.

"Good, aren't they?" said Barney.

Hurly did one last somersault and landed
on Burly's head. Burly leaped off the bicycle.
He bowed to the audience and Hurly fell
off. Everyone laughed and clapped. Burly
ran to Vosta and put his hairy arms round
him. Vosta patted the big chimpanzee and
gave him an apple.

Hurly got over-excited at the shouting and clapping and began to turn somersaults round the ring at a terrific rate, making peculiar noises. Then he scampered round on all fours.

Something landed on his back. It was Miranda, seeing a chance for a ride! Burly snatched her off Hurly's back and began to nurse her in his arms, making little crooning noises.

"Ladies and gentlemen, the show is now over!" shouted Vosta, seeing that nobody made a move. Nobody wanted to, because the chimpanzees and Miranda were so funny!

But the tent was cleared at last and Vosta came up to the children, carrying Miranda. He was very fond of her too. She was busy pulling his tie undone, chattering without stopping.

"Hello, folks," said Vosta. "What do you think of my chimps?"

"They're champs – absolutely champion," said Snubby, making one of his frightful jokes.

"And you're a chump, a champion chump," said Roger, joining in. "I say, Mr Vosta, how did you teach your chimps to ride a bike?"

"Didn't have to teach them," said Vosta. "They saw me riding mine one day, and when I put it down Hurly got on it and rode off straightaway. Then Burly had a go. Like to have tea with us this afternoon?"

"Oh, yes," said all three. Diana turned to Barney. "What about you? Can you, Barney?"

"Yes. I'll get Young Un to come across again," said Barney. "Well, I must be getting back to my stall. Going on the roundabout, Snubby? Don't you get Jimmy to run it too fast again, or you'll get into trouble. I can see old Tonnerre's got his eye on you today."

Tonnerre was with his elephants, watching the children and Loony. He shouted to them in his enormous voice.

"You come to ride on my fine elephants, yes, no?"

But they didn't ride on the elephants. "I'd rather go on the roundabout," said Snubby. "It's not so sway-about as the elephants. Come on, Loony."

They spent a pleasant afternoon, and went to every stall. They saw Brilliant the juggler, they watched the hoopla, with Miranda gathering up the rings so deftly, they went to the skittles and threw balls to knock them down for prizes.

Diana was the only one who managed to knock down three skittles and win a prize. The boy in charge of the skittles waved his hand towards a pile of prizes.

"Take what you like, Miss. Nice to see a

girl beat her brothers. Shouldn't have thought it!"

That made Roger and Snubby immediately pay to throw some more balls, of course, just as the boy had meant them to. He winked at Diana.

"Not so good as you yet, see, Miss? Only knocked one skittle down between them. Poor shots, aren't they?"

Diana looked at the pile of prizes. She chose a small toy dog, much to the boys' surprise. Roger teased her about it.

"Baby! Fancy choosing that! Why didn't you take that little blue vase?"

"I've chosen it for a purpose," said Diana. "You wait and see!"

"Pity there's nothing for Loony to go in for," said Snubby. "I bet he'd win like anything."

"He'd win a rabbit-hole scratching competition," said Roger. "I never did see a dog scratch so fast at a rabbit-hole as he does."

"Or with so little result!" said Diana. "What he'd do if he really came upon a rabbit in a hole I can't imagine. Probably back out in a frightful hurry!"

"Woof," said Loony, knowing they were talking about him. Snubby patted his silky head.

"They're saying horrid things about you," he said. "Never mind. You're the best dog ever! A super dog, a real smasher."

"There's Mr Vosta calling us," said Diana. "He says he's going to have tea. Get the things out of the backpacks, Roger – we'll share them. And I'll tell Barney to come along now if he can."

They all went to Vosta's caravan. Inside was a small table spread with a marvellous tea – and sitting at it already were Hurly and Burly, wearing bibs!

"Get up, chaps, and bow!" said Vosta, and the two chimps rose and bowed politely.

"This is going to be fun!" said Diana, and she was right!

15

A Nice Afternoon – and a Sudden Ending

It was rather a hilarious tea-party, because Miranda and Loony were there too. Miranda behaved really badly – like a spoilt child. She snatched at this and that, she took things off Burly's plate, and she teased Loony unmercifully.

"Miranda! I'll give you to Tonnerre to deal with if I have any more nonsense!" said Barney sternly.

"Oh, let her do what she wants to," said Snubby, delighted. "She's frightfully funny like this. Look – she's picking all the cherries out of the cake now."

Hurly reached out a hairy paw and smacked Miranda sharply. He liked cherries too! Miranda made little crying noises and Burly reached out his paws and picked her up, cradling her against his red-striped jersey. Hurly at once pulled her tail, which lay across his plate.

Burly then punched Hurly, and Vosta hammered on the table. "Behave yourselves!

Don't you know how to behave when visitors are here?"

The chimpanzees looked ashamed. Hurly hid his face behind his hands. The children squealed with laughter.

The tea was excellent – a peculiar mixture, but very appetising.

"It's the sort of tea I like," said Snubby, pleased. "Potted meat and bread and butter, and tinned pineapple and cream, and cherry cake and biscuits, and our own tomato sandwiches and jam tarts."

"And there's ham here too, if you'd like it," said Vosta hospitably.

Snubby did. It was amazing what he could put away when he really liked a meal. The others did their best but he outdid them all. Vosta grinned to see him munching away happily. He liked Snubby, and he loved Loony.

Loony lay with his head on Vosta's foot. Snubby felt quite jealous! It wasn't often Loony did that with anyone.

"Vosta's a magician with animals," said Barney. "He's better with Tonnerre's elephants than Tonnerre is himself."

"Ho, Tonnerre! Br-r-r-r!" said Vosta, unexpectedly. "All those years I have worked for him and still he shouts at me. Br-r-r-r-r-r!"

Burly imitated him: "Br-r-r-r-r-r!" Then he bent down and looked under the table. Loony was near him, his head still on

Vosta's foot. Burly made crooning noises to Loony, who lifted his head and looked astonished.

Burly suddenly disappeared below the table, and put his arms round the surprised spaniel. He tried to lift him up. Loony yelped and snapped, but he did not bite. Snubby rescued him.

"It's all right," said Barney. "Burly is mad about monkeys and dogs and cats – he's got a nursemaid side of himself, I think – wants to nurse them all. Vosta, show us Burly's collection of toy animals."

Vosta opened a cupboard. Inside were a good number of toy animals – a teddy bear, a tiny monkey, two pink cats, a hippo, and a few others. Burly carefully gathered them in his arms.

He set them out on the tea-table, his eyes watchful in case anyone tried to take them from him. But nobody did. They were his toys, precious to him. They watched him arrange them to his liking.

Then Miranda snatched the teddy bear and was off to the top of the caravan with it at once, sitting by the ventilator, chattering. Burly leaped up, growling strangely, Vosta forced him back.

"Stop it now. Silly of me to have let him have his toys out with Miranda there. Barney, can you get the bear back before there's trouble?"

Barney went out of the caravan and called sternly to Miranda, who was still by the ventilator.

Burly made a miserable, howling noise. Diana felt sorry for him. She remembered something she had brought for him and felt in her pocket for the little toy dog she had won for a prize at the skittle match. She held it out to Burly.

He looked at it in surprise. He sat up and reached out a paw for it. He took it very gently and set it down on the table, still keeping hold of it. He stroked it with his other paw and crooned to it. He was a strange chimpanzee!

He forgot about the bear that Miranda had taken. He gave his whole attention to the little toy dog.

"He loves it," said Vosta. "That was nice of you, Diana. He's all right now – forgotten about the bear. Good thing too. I thought he was going to turn nasty for a minute."

Burly took up the toy dog and looked at Vosta, making a deep chattering noise as if he were talking. Vosta understood.

"Yes, it's yours, Burly," he said. "Yours. You can put it with your other toys."

Burly gathered all the toys up and put them back in the cupboard. Barney came in at that moment with the teddy bear. Burly took it, and put that in the cupboard too.

He placed the little dog in the very front.

Vosta shut the cupboard and rubbed Burly affectionately on the head. "Funny fellow, ain't you? Isn't this a nice girl to bring you a present like that?"

Burly understood. He put out a big hand and stroked Diana gently on the arm, making a funny crooning sound as he did so.

"He's thanking you," said Vosta. "And now look at poor old Hurly – he feels left out of all this!"

Hurly was stretching out both hands as if to say; "What about me? I haven't had anything!"

"I've brought him some sweets," said Snubby, remembering, and felt in his pocket. Roger began to feel in his too. "I got him some chocolate," he said.

But neither of the boys found the sweets or chocolate. They were puzzled. "I've lost the sweets," said Snubby. "Blast!"

Barney smiled his wide smile. "I guess Mr Vosta can find them for you. Watch!"

Vosta spoke sternly to Hurly. "Hurly! Turn out your pockets. Go on, you heard what I said – your pockets!"

Hurly made a whimpering sound and stood up. He pulled at his pockets. Vosta slipped his hand in, and out came a bag of sweets and a bar of chocolate!

"He's a pickpocket when there's any sweets around," said Vosta. "Can't blame him. He's only a chimp and he doesn't really know right from wrong when it comes to things like honesty. Bad boy, Hurly! Very bad!"

Hurly hid his face behind his hands again. But he peeped over them, his bright eyes looking at Vosta.

"Give them back to him, Mr Vosta," said Snubby. "He's an awful dear. They both are. Gosh, I wish I had a couple of chimps of my own. It's the first thing I shall buy when I'm grown up."

"It will be fine to see three chimps walking together down the road," said Vosta solemnly, and laughed to see Snubby's indignant face.

"Hello – Tonnerre's taken his elephants off somewhere," said Barney, when the tea-party was over and the little company climbed down the steps of the caravan to the grassy field.

"He's probably taken them to Rilloby," said Vosta. "That's where we go tomorrow. He sometimes takes his elephants the day before we leave. They are so slow in their walking."

Snubby pricked up his ears. If Tonnerre had gone for the evening, it would be a good idea to snoop round his caravan a bit – look in at the window, or at the door – see if there was a safe there that valuable papers could be kept in, perhaps.

He didn't say anything to the others. He wanted to snoop by himself – and anyway three or four people would be noticed at once round a caravan. He waited till Roger and Diana had gone on the roundabout again and then he set off to Tonnerre's big caravan.

Loony went with him, puzzled by the sudden "hists" and "pssts" that Snubby suddenly addressed to him. He trotted at his heels obediently. He liked the fair. It was full of astonishing smells, and amazing animals. He didn't much like the mongrel dogs though, and kept strictly to himself where they were concerned.

Snubby came to Tonnerre's caravan. No one seemed to be about. He looked underneath it. It was hung with all kind of things below – but then, so were all the other caravans. The underneath of a caravan was a convenient place to put a lot of things not wanted for a time.

He stood on a wheel and peeped in at a window; but the curtain was drawn and he couldn't see inside. He went to the other side of the caravan. Ah – the curtain was not drawn across there. He could see in quite well.

Snubby took a good, long look. It seemed a fairly ordinary caravan really – a bunk for a bed, a table that folded down, a heater in one corner – a chair and a stool.

But what was that under the bunk? Snubby could see something sticking out a little. It looked like a black box – a good big one.

Would precious papers be kept in there? The more he looked at the box the more he felt certain that it was full of stolen papers!

He decided to go round to the door and see if it had been left unlatched. But it hadn't, of course. It was locked. Snubby bent to peep through the keyhole to see if he could get another view of that big black box.

Three things happened at exactly the same moment! Loony gave a terrific growl. Somebody gave a tremendous yell that almost deafened Snubby – and a hand came down to grab his collar!

Snubby yelled and fell off the caravan steps. Loony yelped too, as the hand dealt him a slap. Snubby caught sight of a giant-like figure about to grab him again, and he rolled over quickly, jumped up and fled.

An enormous voice came after him. "YOU! COME HERE! I'LL TEACH YOU TO PRY! YES!"

It was Tonnerre. He had only taken his elephants for a little walk down the lane and back – and had just caught Snubby nicely.

He tore after Snubby and Loony, shouting. Everyone stared. Roger and Diana saw Snubby shoot past like a bullet out of a gun, with Loony at his heels. After them came Tonnerre, black as thunder, yelling for all he was worth.

"Gosh – we'd better go," said Roger. "Come on, Di, slip round to the back of the stall, and we'll get behind the caravans and creep down to the gate. What in the world has that idiot of a Snubby done? See you at Rilloby tomorrow, Barney – I hope!"

16

A Morning at the Castle

Snubby had a bad time from the others that evening. "Messing things up! Putting Tonnerre against us! Even perhaps putting him on his guard!" raged Roger on the way home. "What do you want to go snooping round his caravan like that for?"

"It's just the sort of crazy thing that Snubby would do," said Diana. "Making everyone stare. I don't feel as if I want to go to the fair any more."

"Oh, shut up," said Snubby, angry with the others and angry with himself too. "Going on and on at me. I tell you I thought Tonnerre had gone off to Rilloby with his elephants. Anyway, I wasn't doing any harm."

"Harm! You keep on doing harm!" said Roger. "What with your silly Green Hands Gang, and your blabbing about the possibility of a theft at Ricklesham, and now this snooping round Tonnerre's caravan."

There was a silence as the three rode on

down the road. Snubby was really very much upset about it all. "He went off like a crack of thunder," he said last. "And I got a frightful earful."

"Not nearly frightful enough," said Roger at once, and Snubby gave up trying to make peace. Let them be as cross as they liked! He still had old Loony. Loony never raged at him or nagged him or thought badly of him. Never.

Great-uncle Robert was not back from town when they arrived home. Snubby was glad. Now he wouldn't have to go dodging about all evening to avoid him. They had their supper with Mr and Mrs Lynton, and then Snubby wandered off alone with Loony. The others still looked annoyed with him.

Great-uncle came back about half past nine. Snubby, bored, had retired to bed. Roger and Diana were just about to go.

"Had a good day, Uncle Robert?" said Mrs Lynton, taking his coat and scarf from him.

"Yes. Most interesting, my dear, most interesting," said Uncle Robert. "And I've got a nice bit of news for the children. Where are they?"

They were in the lounge, clearing up their things. "Well, my dears," said Great-uncle, beaming at them. "I managed to get in touch with Lord Marloes this morning. And

144

he's given me permission to take you to his castle and see his collection of rare papers and interesting animals. We'll go tomorrow, if you like."

"Oh, thanks, Great-uncle! That's great!" said Diana. Roger beamed too. Now they would be able to have a look round before the thief came – if he meant to come!

"I thought you'd be pleased," said Great-uncle. "I'm pleased myself. I haven't seen his collection for years. It will refresh my memory nicely."

Mrs Lynton looked slightly astonished. She went out into the hall with Diana and Roger when they left the room to go up to bed.

"Do you really want to go looking at dull old papers?" she said. "Because you will find them terribly dull, you know – and dear old Uncle Robert can be a bit of a bore when he's explaining them. I know because he often took me with him when I was a girl."

"It's all right, Mother – we shall love it," Diana assured her. "It's really the stuffed animals we want to see. There's quite a good collection of them there."

"Oh well – you go if you like," said her mother. "It will please your great-uncle tremendously."

It certainly did! He set off with them at ten o'clock the next morning in a specially

145

hired car, smiling all over his face. He was so pleased about the little expedition that he quite forgot that for the last two days he had wanted to talk to Snubby about something important!

Loony, alas, was not allowed to come. "I'm sorry, but no dogs are allowed in the castle," said Great-uncle, quite determined in no circumstance to take Loony. Loony had only to see Great-uncle to take it into his head to sit down and scratch himself violently – and the old man wasn't going to have him indulging in a prolonged scratch in the car!

They arrived at the castle. It was not really a very large one, more like a big mansion in fact. The big iron gates at the entrance to the drive were opened by the lodge-keeper, who came out of his little lodge nearby.

"Your pass, please, sir," he said, and Great-uncle gave it to him.

"That's all right, sir," said the man. "Quite busy this morning, we are! Yours is the third pass I've checked today. Well, we've got a nice little museum up there – and be sure to look at the albino badger, sir. I found him myself! His lordship was downright pleased with me."

"We'll have a look at it," said Great-uncle, and the car went on up the drive to a large front door. A butler opened it, and the pass was shown once more.

"This way, sir," said the butler, in a voice as pompous as Great-uncle's. Snubby nudged Diana and she smiled. She knew what Snubby was thinking.

The man took them down a stone-floored hall, and up a vast flight of marble stairs that swept round in a magnificent curve to the floor above.

They went up to another floor, and the man led the way to a small wing built off from the main part of the house. He unlocked a big wooden door that led into a dark stone passage. Another door stood at the end. He unlocked that too.

It led into a big room that was lined with books from ceiling to floor.

On they went, through the room to the other side, where a small, stout door was let into the wall. This was unlocked by two different keys!

"You keep the place well locked," said Roger. "Two locked doors, and now a third one, double-locked! You don't mean burglars to get in!"

"No, sir," said the butler. "His lordship prizes his collection greatly. Here you will find the stuffed animals, sir, and beyond, on those shelves, are the papers. Before you leave, sir, I must ask you to wait while Mr Johns, the custodian, checks the collection. We have to do that, sir, otherwise it would be easy for people to put something valuable in their pockets – there are plenty of dishonest people about these days!"

"That's all right," said Great-uncle. "Check all you like. It's good to see such care taken of a valuable collection. There have been so many thefts lately."

"Yes, sir," said the butler and locked them into the room!

"We're locked in!" said Diana, half-alarmed.

"That's quite usual," said Great-uncle. "It's just a sensible precaution. We have to ring that bell when we are ready to go. Hello – there's somebody else here."

There were two people – one an old, old man who was so bent that it was quite impossible to see his face. The other was a younger man with a beard and very bushy eyebrows indeed. He had a moustache, and was altogether a most hairy-looking person.

"He's even got hairs growing out of his ears!" whispered Snubby to Diana. "Like eyebrows!"

"Sh! He'll hear you," said Diana crossly. Snubby's whispers were always much too loud.

The two men were examining the various papers set out and labelled on the shelves. The bearded man glanced round at the new-comers and then lost interest in them. He turned the pages of a manuscript carefully over and over, as the children wandered round.

"Di! You go and listen to Great-uncle Robert and we'll have a look round," whispered Roger. "I'll make a rough plan of the room – just in case, you know!"

Diana went with Great-uncle and began to ask him questions. The old man began a lengthy explanation of this manuscript and that one. Diana was very bored. She hardly understood a word. She looked round for the boys. They were walking all round, looking here and there. They were not really very thrilled with the stuffed animals, which were a poor, mangy-looking lot, some with the moth in their furry coats.

The white badger was there, looking extremely dirty. There were two foxes with a litter of cubs, all stuffed and standing together, looking very unnatural. There was a pole-cat with one eye. The other had apparently dropped out at some time and had not been put back. There were two squirrels, outside what was supposed to be their nest. The very moth-eaten head of a young squirrel peeped over the edge of the dusty nest.

"I don't think much of these," said Snubby, disgusted. "They must be animals Lord Marloes stuffed when he was a boy, and was so proud of them that he couldn't bear to part with them. They're horrible."

"What's that fellow doing?" whispered
Roger suddenly to Snubby, nudging him.
Snubby looked at the man with the beard.
He was laying something down on one of
the manuscripts, moving it up and down the
page.

"It's only a magnifying-glass, idiot," said
Snubby. "You've seen Great-uncle using one
on his old papers. Don't be so suspicious!"

Roger looked a bit crestfallen. He turned
to look at the bent old man. How could
anyone be so bent! It must be dreadful.

Even when he walked from shelf to shelf he was so bent that he was forced to look down at the floor all the time.

Roger was glad when the two men rang the bell and went. The custodian, a wrinkled old man, came in, shut the door, and went rapidly through the papers on the shelves to make sure they were all there. He didn't even glance at the animals!

"I expect he hopes somebody will steal them some day, the horrible moth-eaten things," said Snubby, as the two men went out with the custodian. The door was once more double-locked.

"Now I'm going to make a sketch of the room," said Roger. "Just in case!"

"Put in the other two locked doors leading to the room," said Snubby, watching Roger beginning to draw. "Oh, you're doing it awfully well. What are those – windows?"

"Yes. They're well and truly fastened. Did you notice?" said Roger. "And they've got bars outside too. Nobody could get in there."

He looked up to see if there was a skylight, but there wasn't. He sketched in where the shelves were put and put dots for the stuffed animals on the floor. He marked where the chairs were, a desk, the fireplace, and a small table on which stood some kind of plant.

It really was quite a good drawing. Roger

felt rather pleased. Snubby admired it whole-heartedly.

They glanced at poor Diana. She was looking rather pale, having been standing beside Great-uncle for about an hour, listening wearily to a lecture she didn't understand and didn't like.

"Poor old Di!" said Roger under his breath to Snubby. "She looks fed up. Shall we go and take her place?"

"No," said Snubby firmly. "You can if you want to. I'm not going to. I should be sick."

"Well, go and be sick," said Roger. "Great-uncle would take us all out then. You couldn't be sick in here."

Snubby caught sight of something on the broad mantelpiece. It was a clock. The hands pointed to half past eleven. Snubby tiptoed over to it, opened the front of the clock and turned the hands till they said half past twelve. Roger gave a snort of laughter, which he hurriedly turned into a sneeze.

Snubby went up to Great-uncle Robert. "Er – Great-uncle – I just hate to interrupt you – but do you think it's time to go? The clock on the mantelpiece says half past twelve."

"Bless us all! How time flies!" said Great-uncle in amazement, and rang the bell for the custodian. "Incredible! Quite incredible!"

17

The Fair Moves to Rilloby

They went home in the car, Roger longing to show Diana his really excellent drawing. Great-uncle rambled on, unable to stop. The children listened, bored, wishing they were home.

"Thanks awfully, Great-uncle," said Roger politely. "We've had a wizard morning."

"A what morning?" asked Great-uncle, puzzled.

"Wizard. Smashing. Super," explained Snubby. "Thanks a lot."

"I'm very glad, very glad." Great-uncle beamed, thinking what nice interesting children they were all of a sudden. He really must take them to some other collection some time. "Now you'd better go and get tidy for lunch," he said. "Dear me – I hope your mother won't think I've brought you back too late."

Considering that it was only ten to twelve, and not ten to one, as Great-uncle thought, Mrs Lynton thought they were back very early, not late. As for Great-uncle, he was simply amazed to find what a long time there was until lunch! He couldn't understand it at all.

Roger showed his map to Diana. "Now," he said, "if there's a burglary we shall have a map of the whole place. It may be very, very useful."

Loony was so pleased to see them again that he had one of his mad fits, rushing up and down the stairs at top speed, in and out of all the bedrooms, sending mats flying this way and that. Sardine was scared out of her life and fled to the top of the grandfather clock, where she sat swinging her tail like a pendulum till Loony's madness had exhausted itself.

Great-uncle locked himself into his bedroom when he realised that Loony was having a mad fit. That dog! If he wasn't barking, he was scratching, and if he wasn't scratching, he was going mad. The only really satisfactory dogs were stuffed ones, Great-uncle thought. At least they didn't scratch!

The children didn't go to see Barney that day, partly because Mr Lynton was at home and told them all to come out into the garden and help him with some trees he was chopping down; and partly because they knew the fair was moving to Rilloby, and they thought that Barney might be too busy

154

to want them around that day.

Snubby had a third reason. He thought it would be wise to allow Tonnerre to forget what had happened. He meant to give Tonnerre a very wide berth in future!

Barney turned up himself that evening with Miranda on his shoulder. He waited in the garden till he saw Roger. Then he whistled his low clear whistle.

Roger turned. "That you, Barney?" he called. "Oh, good! Had any supper? We've had ours, but we can easily ask Mrs Harris for something for you."

"I wouldn't mind a bit of cake," said Barney, who had had very little to eat that day in the move to Rilloby.

"Come to the back door. We'll ask Mrs Harris for something," said Roger. They appeared at the back door and Mrs Harris gave a shriek to see Miranda.

"Land sakes! Is it a monkey? Don't you dare to let it come into the kitchen. Whatever next!"

However, she calmed down enough to cut poor hungry Barney some sandwiches and gave him a big chunk of treacle tart. He held up a sandwich to Miranda and she delicately took out a bit of tomato from the middle and ate it.

"A monkey now! What next!" said Mrs Harris.

"You come to Rilloby Fair and you'll see

a couple of chimpanzees," said Roger. "You should see them ride their bicycle."

"Now that I don't believe," said Mrs Harris. "All right, I'll come and if I see two chimpanzees riding bicycles, well, I'll eat my best Sunday hat."

"You look out – you'll have to go to church in your second best hat now – you'll have eaten your best one," said Roger, with a grin.

Barney hadn't any news except that they had moved the fair successfully to Dolling Hill at Rilloby, and that Tonnerre seemed to have recovered his temper and had spent a happy afternoon spring-cleaning his two elephants.

"Spring-cleaning them! What do you mean?" said Diana, who had joined them with Snubby.

"Oh, he gets a stepladder, and a can of oil, and a brush – and he oils the creases in their skins and rubs them all over," said Barney, eating the sandwiches very fast indeed. "He loves that job. It's put him into quite a good temper."

"I can hardly sit down, where I fell down the caravan steps," said Snubby.

"Serves you right," said Diana. "If you always got what you always deserve, you'd always never be able to sit down."

"I don't like that remark," said Snubby, having worked it out bit by bit. But by that time Roger was showing Barney his map of the room in the castle and nobody took any notice of him.

"How are Hurly and Burly?" asked Diana. "Do they get upset with a move?"

"Not a bit," said Barney, giving Miranda a tiny piece of treacle tart. "Oh, you little nuisance – you've dropped it down my neck!"

"What – the treacle?" said Diana sympathetically. "How awful."

That reminded Roger of something. "Would you like a bath?" he asked Barney. "Mum says you can have one any time."

Barney hesitated. "Well – I'd awfully like one now if she really means it. I'm filthy with all the moving today. I just can't seem to get clean in cold water, and that's all I get."

So Barney was escorted to the bathroom, where he stared at the great cream-coloured bath, quite overcome. Diana brought him a thick cream-coloured towel, a very big one.

"What's this?" he asked, thinking it was a bed-quilt or something. He was astonished when she told him it was only a towel. His towel was usually a very dirty rag of a handkerchief. How he enjoyed that hot bath! Miranda sat on the cold tap and looked on in amazement. What could Barney be doing in water that smoked? She cautiously put one small foot down into it

157

and curled it up with a squeal.

"Did it bite you?" asked Barney, soaping himself all over, and replacing the soap in its dish. Miranda took it up and smelled it. She nibbled it and flung the soap into the water in disgust. She spat out the bit she had nibbled.

"Miranda, that's not nice behaviour in a bathroom like this," said Barney. "Now where's the soap gone?"

He hunted in the water for it and then lay peacefully in the warmth. Loony scratched at the door.

"Sorry. The bathroom's occupied, Loony," murmured Barney, half asleep. Then he heard the voices of the others outside in the garden and he sat up, reaching for the wonderful towel.

It was a lovely night, and the children walked back to the fair with Barney in the moonlight. Miranda couldn't understand Barney's sweet-scented smell. It didn't seem like Barney! She sat on Snubby's shoulder all the way, hoping Barney's nice Barney-smell would come back to him.

As they came to the gate of the field where the fair was being held, someone came out. It was Tonnerre, all by himself. Snubby recognised him at once and hid quickly in the hedge. The others walked boldly on.

"Evening, sir," said Barney politely.

Tonnerre peered at him.

"Oh, it's you. Give an eye to my elephants, will you, when you get in? Young Un's with them now, but they're restless – they don't like a move."

"Yes, sir," said Barney. "Will you be long?"

"No. Just one hour," said Tonnerre. "Going down the road and back."

Roger pulled Barney to him. "Where's he really going? You go on into the field. I'll follow him and see where he's going. You never know!"

Barney nodded and went through the gate. Snubby detached himself from the hedge. He had heard Roger's whisper.

"I say – are we really going to follow Tonnerre?" he asked excitedly. "Loony would be awfully good at following his track if we lost it."

"He won't follow it because he's jolly well not coming," said Roger. "Nor are you. You take Di home. I'll do the tracking! Go on now, Snubby. I must get after him, or I'll lose him."

He left the other two and ran down the lane. Where was Tonnerre going? Was he really only going down the road and back?

He came to a fork and saw Tonnerre's figure in the distance, enormous in the moonlight.

"Oho!" said Roger to himself. "He's taken the turning to Marloes Castle. Now what do you think of that?"

18

Snubby Enjoys Himself

Tonnerre strode on down the road, right in the very middle of it, his shadow black behind him. Roger followed. Marloes Castle was, by the signpost, half a mile away – not very far from Rilloby Fair! Roger kept close to the hedge, not wanting Tonnerre to see him.

He felt excited. What was Tonnerre going to do? Surely he wasn't going to commit any kind of robbery at that time of night? It was early, surely, for thieves!

"If I see him shin up over the wall, or do any other funny business, I shall call the police somehow or other," thought Roger. "I'd better notice where the nearest house is because I could go and ask to use their telephone. Gosh, this is exciting!"

He thought of the room in the little separate wing of the castle, protected by two locked doors and a third one double-locked. Windows fastened and barred. Well, well, if Tonnerre could go through all those, leaving them still locked and fastened, he was a very clever man indeed!

Tonnerre walked on and on. Roger kept well back in the shadows at the side of the lane. Tonnerre did not turn to see if anyone was following him. He simply walked straight on.

Marloes Castle loomed up in the distance. It had a high wall all round it. Its windows gleamed in the moonlight. Roger tried to see the barred window of the room where the stuffed animals and valuable old papers were kept. He spotted it at last. How on earth could a great fellow like Tonnerre climb up a sheer, straight wall, and get through barred windows?

Tonnerre did nothing of the sort, of course. He came to the big iron gates, and there he stopped for the first time. He peered through at Marloes Castle, his great arms holding on to the gates as he looked this way and that.

Roger held his breath. What was going to happen now?

It was all very disappointing. Nothing happened at all. Tonnerre simply went on walking round the walls of the grounds, arrived at the iron gates again, and went back by the way he had come!

"Well!" thought Roger. "What a long walk I've had for nothing! All the same, perhaps Tonnerre was looking to see how he could get in some other night. Making his plans. Yes, that's it, I expect. He means to come back some other night and get in. But how does he mean to do it? It beats me!"

Roger saw Tonnerre safely back to the fair field, and then went home. Mrs Lynton was cross with him for being so late. "The others have been in for a long time," she said, "and have gone up to bed. Do you know it's ten o'clock? I'm surprised at you, Roger. I suppose you've been with Barney – but do remember that although I like him very much, I shall not allow you to keep the hours he does."

"Sorry, Mum," said Roger, and said no more. He couldn't possibly explain about Tonnerre.

The others were very disappointed when they heard that all that Tonnerre had done was to peer through the gates of the castle and walk round the walls.

"Still, I think you're right when you say he was looking round and laying his plans," said Diana. "Goodnight! We'll talk about it again tomorrow."

They all went to the fair again the next day, after it had opened. They saw Mrs Harris there, having an afternoon off. Snubby went over to her.

"Got your best Sunday hat out, ready to eat?" he said. "You'll see the two chimps riding their bicycle this afternoon. Come on

– I'll buy your ticket. I've never seen anybody eat their hat, and I'd just love to see you gobble yours."

"Go on with you now," said Mrs Harris. She went with all of them into the tent where Hurly and Burly gave their performances. Vosta nodded to them, and gave Mrs Harris a front seat. She was very pleased.

Her eyes nearly fell out of her head when she saw Hurly and Burly doing their tricks, and when they rode the bicycle round and round the grass ring, Burly on the pedals first, with Hurly on the bars, and then the other way about, she exclaimed in wonder.

"Well, I never did! Well, I never did in all my life! Well, who would have thought of that now! Well, of all the extraordinary things!"

Snubby grinned. "You'll have to eat your words as well as your hat. When can I come and see you at your meal, Mrs Harris? And do you eat your hat with a knife and fork, or just chew it?"

"Get away with your nonsense now," said Mrs Harris in a daze, watching the chimpanzees going head-over-heels without stopping. "It fair makes me dizzy watching them do that."

"Yes, but what about your Sunday hat?" persisted Snubby. "You can't go back on your word, you know."

Mrs Harris began to feel uncomfortable. "Go on now, you know a hat can't be eaten," she said. "You let me off, you little pest, and I'll make you some more meringues. Oh, my goodness, what are the creatures doing now? Tell this one to go away – I don't like its hairy face!"

Hurly had come up to Snubby, grinning all over his funny face. He patted Snubby, and then, as Mrs Harris appeared to be Snubby's friend, he patted her too. She rose from her chair and fled out of the tent, scared and trembling.

"Well, there now, I never did in my life!" she kept saying to herself. "I never did!"

Snubby wondered what it was she never did. He followed her and reminded her of her bargain.

"Remember – either you eat your hat or I eat your meringues!"

"You're a caution, you are," said Mrs Harris. "You keep away from me now. I want to enjoy myself. You and your hats and meringues!"

Snubby kept carefully out of Tonnerre's sight. He kept as far from his caravan as possible too. He didn't want another deafening earful! He saw the others by the hoopla stall and went to have a word with them. "Mrs Harris isn't going to eat her best Sunday hat – she'll make us some meringues instead."

"Good work!" said Roger. "Hello – here comes Old Ma. Wonder what she wants."

Old Ma came up to the hoopla stall. Her bright bird-like eyes darted all round. She spoke to Barney.

"You seen Young Un anywhere, Barney? I want him to come and watch my pot for me. I got to do some washing and I can't do both."

"He's gone to help with the elephants," said Barney. "There's such a lot of people here today that Mr Tonnerre can't cope with everyone that wants rides. There he is, look. Billy Tell's got the shooting-range."

"Never anyone to help Old Ma," muttered the old woman, and turned to go.

"I'll come along and stir up your pot," said Snubby, thinking it might be interesting to talk to the old woman.

"You! The only thing you'll ever stir up is trouble!" said Old Ma, and went off into a cackle of laughter. "All right, you come along then – and you can get me some water from the stream. I've not got enough."

Snubby found that he had taken on more than he bargained for. He had to fetch various pails of water from the stream first of all, then he had to fetch more wood for the fire, and then stand and stir the big iron pot with a long iron spoon whose handle got hotter and hotter.

"What's in here?" asked Snubby, peering into the bubbling liquid.

"Ah, don't you ask no questions and you won't get no lies," answered the old woman, now busy washing clothes in a tub. Snubby grinned. By the smell it seemed as if rabbit, hare, a chicken or two and possibly a duck were all in the big pot. Snubby felt that he wouldn't at all mind having a plateful of the delicious-smelling concoction.

Ma began to talk as she washed. Snubby listened, fascinated. She talked about Bill Tell and Vosta and many others he didn't know – Presto the conjurer, Sticky Stanley the clown, Mr Volla and his horses, Madame Petronella and her parrots – people in other circuses and fairs, people she had known and had never forgotten. Out came the names in a never-ending stream, all with some story attached to them.

"What about Mr Tonnerre?" ventured Snubby. "Have you known him long?"

"Long! Too long! Ah, that man's temper. It doesn't bear thinking about," said Old Ma, rinsing a peculiar-looking garment in her tub. "Always he had a temper, always he was shouting, always he was big – but what a wonderful acrobat! Ah, to see him on the tightrope – why, he could dance better on that than most men on a dance floor."

Snubby was amazed. Tonnerre an acrobat! How very extraordinary. He didn't look a bit like one. He was so big and heavy and yet, when Snubby thought of it, he walked very lightly and softly when he wanted to – as he must have walked when he caught Snubby snooping round his caravan!

Snubby remembered how easily and lightly he leaped up to the necks of his elephants when he wanted to, too. Yes – he must have been a fine acrobat.

"Does he do any – er – acrobating – now?" asked Snubby.

"Who? Tonnerre?" Old Ma gave a squeal of laughter. "That fat old man! He is nothing but an elephant now – but still he can walk the tightrope, and he can leap his own height from the ground. But the strongest thing about Tonnerre now is his temper. He is afraid of nothing, that one – nothing but one thing."

"And that's you, isn't it, Old Ma?" said Snubby with a grin. "I say, how long have I got to stir this stuff? The smell is so super that I can't stand it much longer unless I keep licking the spoon."

Old Ma cackled again. She liked Snubby and his cheek. "You stay and have dinner with Old Ma," she said. "Just you and that dog of yours. What's his name now? Snubby, isn't it? And yours is Loony. Well, well – whoever named you was a clever one!"

"Here, Ma, you've got it all wrong," protested Snubby, leaping out of the way as Old Ma emptied her tub of soapy water much too near him.

"Mind out, Loony," she said to him, and both dog and boy minded out. "No, you set yourself down and wait a minute and I'll give you the best meal you've ever tasted in your life. Old Ma knows how to cook, she does!"

19

More Doings of Snubby

The others were quite jealous when they saw Old Ma ladling out an enormous plateful from her iron pot and presenting it to Snubby.

"Look at that now," said Barney in amazement and envy. "Never seen Old Ma so generous before. How does Snubby do it? Getting supper from Old Ma and meringues out of your Mrs Harris, and . . ."

"Just pure cheek," said Roger. "Gosh, look, Old Ma's putting a plate down for Loony too. How wild all those mongrels look, sitting in a ring there, watching!"

Snubby came over to the others at last, looking very satisfied with himself and his supper. Loony looked more than satisfied. He looked extremely fat and developed a fit of hiccups at once.

"Stop it," said Snubby severely. "Hiccups mean you've been overeating. Don't give yourself away like that, Loony!"

Loony did another hiccup and looked

surprised. Sneezes and hiccups always surprised him. They were so sudden and seemed to belong to him in some mysterious way that he couldn't understand. He sat down and began to nod, feeling full and comfortable.

Snubby suddenly got the hiccups too, and retired to get over them, annoyed at the laughter and remarks of the others. He decided to buy some sweets for Hurly and Burly. He could see Vosta walking them round the field, holding them by their hands, one on each side of him. They loved a walk like that, when there were plenty of people to see.

Vosta brought them over to the hoopla stall. Miranda chattered to the two chimpanzees, showing them the row of wooden rings she had pushed up her left arm ready to hand out to customers. Hurly held out a hand for some.

"No, you don't," said Barney swiftly.

"Why not?" asked Roger.

"Well, he rings everything in sight," said Barney. "Never misses. And then he makes such a clamour for the things he's ringed. He's as cute as can be."

"Oh, do let's see him!" begged Diana. Snubby came up and joined in too. He had a pocketful of cheap sweets for the chimpanzees, and some better ones for himself and the others.

"Go on – let him throw," said Snubby. "I'll pay for the rings for him."

"I'll let him have them for nothing," said Barney. "But don't you let him grab the things he rings like he did last time, Mr Vosta. He smashed one of my clocks."

Hurly threw a ring. It fell exactly over a small doll. He chattered excitedly. Everyone clapped him. He threw another, and that slid beautifully over a little green vase. The third one fell round another toy without touching it. It really was good throwing.

Miranda deftly gathered up the rings and slipped them back on her arm. She held out her hand to Hurly for the money he should have given her for them.

"It's all right. He's not paying," said Barney. "And he's not having the things he ringed either. Take your great hands away, Hurly!"

Hurly was longing to get the things he had ringed. Snubby felt quite sorry for him. It did seem a shame to throw so well and not have any reward. He remembered the sweets he had bought.

He put his hand into his pocket to get the ones he had bought for them – and they were not there, of course!

"Hurly! You've pinched the sweets I bought for you!" he cried, and pulled the chimpanzee's hairy arm. Hurly at once put it round him and hugged him affectionately.

"No. You're a wicked pickpocket," said Snubby severely. "Mr Vosta, I bought some sweets for them both, and they're gone!"

"Hurly. Turn out your pockets!" said Mr Vosta sternly. Hurly whimpered and pulled at one of his pockets. Out came a bag of sweets!

"Bad boy! Naughty boy!" said Vosta. "No more rings for you! No more sweets either!"

"Keep the sweets and give them to Hurly and Burly later on," said Snubby. "I bought them for them. I say, can't you let Burly throw rings too?"

"Yes. But he goes wild after a bit and throws them at everybody," said Vosta. "So we don't encourage him to begin. Come along, Hurly and Burly. We'll go and see Mr Tonnerre and say goodnight to him and his elephants."

The chimpanzees loved the two elephants and went willingly to see them. Snubby roared to see one of the elephants put his trunk round Burly and lift him right to the top of his great head. There sat Burly, swinging to and fro, chattering excitedly.

"I wish I belonged to a fair," said Snubby enviously. "Gosh, wouldn't I like to have a couple of chimps like that. I'd have a string of monkeys too – and some elephants – and I wouldn't mind a horse or two."

"I think we ought to be going home to

supper," said Roger, looking at his watch. "I suppose you can't come too, Barney, tonight?"

"I'd love to," said Barney, "but there's no one to take over my stall, and as you can see, we're pretty busy tonight. Young Un can't take it – he's still with the elephants."

"Bad luck. Come on, Snubby – we shan't get any supper if we don't go now," said Roger.

"I can't face supper tonight," said Snubby dolefully. "Not after Old Ma's helping out of her pot. I just can't face it. I say, Barney – could I take over the hoopla stall for you and you could go and have supper with the others?"

"What will Tonnerre say?" said Barney doubtfully. "I daren't go and ask him. He'll probably run you out of the field if he sees you at the stall."

"I'll go and ask Old Ma," said Snubby suddenly. "Tonnerre's afraid of her. If she says I can, I will."

He went off to where she was hanging out clothes on a line she had put up from caravan to caravan. "Ma," he began, "I'm afraid of asking Mr Tonnerre – so can I ask you instead? Barney wants to go off for a bit. May I take over his stall? I'll do it properly."

"Course you can, Loony," said Old Ma, with a twinkle. "You and your dog Snubby

174

can surely look after a stall for an hour or two. I'll manage Tonnerre if he starts shouting around."

"What's she called you Loony for?" asked Roger, who had followed him. "All right – you needn't tell me. I can guess, it's quite a good idea on her part!"

Snubby scowled. Then he cheered up. He was to have the hoopla stall to himself – that was fine! He'd make a terrific lot of money and show Barney what he could do!

"Shall I leave Miranda to help you?" asked Barney.

"No thanks. I can manage with Loony," said Snubby. "Go on, all of you. Leave me to it. I shall do fine."

They went off and left him, all feeling very hungry. Snubby must indeed have eaten a magnificent meal not to be able to manage two suppers!

Snubby had a good time with the stall. He really let himself go. He tried out the loudest voice he possessed and it really was a pretty good one.

"Walk up, walk up, WALK UP! Walk up, walk up, WALK UP!" he bellowed. "Finest stall in the fair. Clocks, toys, chocs, bowls, spoons, brooches, pins, ring anything you like! Try your skill, try your SKILL! Mothers, come and beat the fathers, sisters, come and beat your brothers, choose what you like and ring it. Come along now! Walk up, walk up, WALK UP!"

People listened in amusement, surprised to see such a small boy in charge of the stall. Snubby was only twelve, and with his snub nose, red hair and masses of freckles, to say nothing of his cheeky grin, he made people smile whenever they looked at him.

They drifted over to the hoopla stall and soon he was doing a brisk business. Loony was very useful. He kept watch for any rings that fell to the ground and picked them up at once. "You're as good as Miranda," Snubby told him, and Loony wagged his stump of a tail, pleased.

Tonnerre soon spotted that it was not Barney in charge of the stall, and he wandered over to see what was up. When he saw Snubby, his face took on its look of black thunder. Snubby saw him and was petrified.

But Old Ma was there at once. "You let him be!" she cried shrilly. "He's doing fine! You lay a finger on him, Tonnerre, and I'll tell you some of the things you did when you were a lad. Yes, I put you across my knee many a time, and you yelled like . . ."

But Tonnerre was gone. He was no match for Old Ma's tongue and he knew it. Anyway, the boy was doing well and taking money. There was no need to interfere. Plenty of time later on to take it out of that snooping little rogue if he wanted to.

Snubby stayed there till Barney came back. The others weren't with him. "Your aunt says you're to go straight back," he told Snubby. "I don't think I ought to have left you here, really. She didn't seem very pleased. Thanks a lot. I say – did you take all that money?"

"Yes. It was easy," boasted Snubby. "And you should have seen Tonnerre turn green when he came up and saw me raking in all that money – more than he's taken all night with his elephants, I bet. He just faded away, and didn't say a word to me. I just looked him in the eye, and—"

"Go on – you didn't do anything of the sort," said Barney, who knew Snubby's little ways very well indeed, by now. "But anyway, thanks very much. I enjoyed my supper and going to your home again."

Snubby remembered the sweets he had

bought for himself and the others. He felt hungry and thought he would like a few. He could give some to Barney too. He put his hand into his pocket – but the sweets weren't there! That tiresome Hurly must have taken them at the same time as he had taken the other bag. Snubby felt annoyed. Really, Hurly might have been content with just one bag! He wasn't only dishonest, he was greedy too!

"I'm just going over to Vosta's caravan to see if Hurly's got some more sweets of mine," said Snubby. "I'll be back."

He went over to the caravan. It was in darkness except for a very small oil-lamp burning on a shelf with a safety ledge. Snubby knocked.

A chattering noise greeted him, and he heard the creaking of bunks. Hurly and Burly slept in the same caravan as Vosta. He would never be separated from them, even at night.

"Are you there, Mr Vosta?" asked Snubby. But Vosta was not there. Only the chimps were there, curled up in their blankets on the small bunks they had. Hurly came to the door and opened it. Both chimpanzees could do ordinary things like that.

"Hurly! Did you take my sweets?" said Snubby severely. "Turn out your pockets!"

But Hurly had no clothes on! He always had to undress at night, and he stood there dressed only in his hairy coat. Loony sniffed at his legs. With a bound Burly was beside them, trying to lift Loony up in his arms.

"Oh, Burly, don't – Loony doesn't like it," said Snubby, trying to rescue poor Loony. "Get back to bed. Go on. Do you hear me?"

To Snubby's surprise, the chimpanzees obeyed him. They got back under their blankets, making a few peculiar noises to one another. Snubby saw their clothes on the floor nearby. He saw that there was a bulge in one of the pockets, and he slipped his hand into it. He pulled out his paper bag of sweets.

"Bad Hurly!" he scolded. "Go to sleep, both of you. I shan't buy you sweets again if you behave like this. Goodnight, you pair of scamps!"

20

A Most Exciting Find

Snubby went over to Barney again, but Barney didn't want any sweets. He had had such a splendid supper, he said!

"Do go home," he begged Snubby. "Your aunt will be so annoyed. She'll never ask me to supper again. Do go, Snubby."

Snubby went. Very fortunately for him, his aunt was phoning somebody, so he simply crept behind her, gave her a kiss and rushed upstairs before she could scold him.

"You're frightfully late, Snubby," said Roger's sleepy voice. "I say, Mum wasn't at all pleased at us leaving you there with the hoopla stall."

Snubby yawned. He suddenly found that he was really very tired. He said a few words to Roger, and fell into bed after a very short wash and a rub-over of his teeth.

It was next morning that he discovered something that excited the three of them so tremendously that they could hardly do their morning tasks!

Snubby overslept. He rushed down late to breakfast, got a scolding from his uncle, and decided that he had better go straight upstairs and make his bed as soon after breakfast as possible, to get out of any further scolding from his aunt.

He stripped his bed. Under the pillow was the bag of sweets he had rescued from Hurly's pocket the night before.

He picked them up, wishing that toffees didn't ooze out and make everything sticky.

Stuck to the bag was a bit of torn paper. Snubby pulled it away without thinking.

There was something written on it, but at first he didn't even bother to read it. Then a word caught his eye.

Castle.

That rang a bell in Snubby's mind immediately, of course, and he smoothed out the dirty, sticky bit of paper at once. Part of two words were there, and the whole of one.

This is what Snubby read:

oes Castle. Midnig

He stared in excitement. He gave such a whistle of surprise that Roger came over and looked at the paper too.

"What's this?" he said. "Where did you get it? Why the excitement?"

"Roger! Hurly stole a bag of sweets last

night and I went to get it out of his pocket in his caravan – and stuck to the bag was this torn bit of paper. It must have been part of a note," said Snubby, his face red with excitement. "See what it says?"

Roger looked at it a lot more carefully. He took it from Snubby, and his face went red too.

"Gosh yes – oes – that's the end of Marloes, I suppose. 'Marloes Castle. Midnight.' That last word must surely be part of 'midnight'. I say, Snubby – we're on to something now!"

182

The two stared at one another, thrilled. Loony whined and scraped at Snubby's leg. What was up?

"Let's tell Di," said Snubby, and they called her. She was as excited as they were.

"Let's work it out," said Roger. "How did this bit of paper get into Hurly's pocket with the sweets to begin with?"

"Well, you know what Hurly is – he picks up anything he sees on the ground," said Snubby. "Or he takes things out of people's pockets. He may have got this from anywhere! Somebody must have torn it up, that's plain – and probably thrown it away on the field. This is just one of the bits."

"Who handed the note out – and who got the note?" wondered Diana. "Or did a messenger come and give it to somebody in the fair? Or did it come by post to somebody, who read it, noted what it said, and tore it up? We can't tell."

"The only thing we do know is that somebody got the note and somebody is going to Marloes Castle at midnight – and we can jolly well guess why!" said Snubby. "I say, isn't this exciting – absolutely super."

"Brilliant," agreed Roger. "I wonder who got the note. Do you suppose the one who got it is to meet the one who sent it?"

"There's only one way of finding out," said Snubby, his eyes shining and his voice solemn. "Only one way. We'll have to go there at midnight ourselves and watch."

There was a silence. "I say, what a thrill!" said Roger. "But we don't know what night. The note only says 'Midnight' – it doesn't say Monday, Tuesday, Wednesday – though the whole note must have, of course."

"Well, we'll go every night then!" said Snubby.

There was another silence. "Anyone know how long the fair's going to be at Rilloby?" said Diana at last.

"Barney says till Wednesday," said Snubby. "And today is Thursday. Five more nights till they go – and on one of them we know there's a robbery going to take place."

"Had we better tell the police, do you think?" asked Diana. The boys looked at her scornfully.

"What! When we're nicely on the track now! Don't be a spoilsport!" said Roger. "Besides, what exactly can we tell the police? About Diana's hunch – our suspicion of Tonnerre – and this torn note? They'd laugh at us."

"Course they would," said Snubby, who couldn't bear the thought of handing over this mystery to anyone else. "Just like a girl to think of the police."

"All right, all right. I don't want to," said Diana. "But I don't see how we can go on watching Marloes Castle for five nights running. We'll be so sleepy we won't be able to do a thing the next day."

"Di, the note says midnight," said Roger, exasperated. "That means the robbery will be done then – and we can go home and go to sleep."

"Pooh – as if we'd any of us go to sleep after seeing a robbery done," said Diana. "All right, I'm not really making difficulties. I'm just seeing what's the best thing to do."

It really was a most exciting thing to discuss. Mrs Lynton couldn't imagine what was the matter with the children that morning – no beds made, no jobs done, even Loony not brushed!

"What mischief are you planning, I should like to know," she said. "Diana, the beds! If they are not made in the next twenty minutes I shall be really cross."

Of course, Barney had to be told. They dashed over to Rilloby Fair as soon as ever they could, and got him into a corner where nobody could possibly hear them, or see the torn bit of paper they handed him.

Barney was amazed. "Well, think of that!" he said. "Diana was right. There is somebody in this fair who's got something to do with the robberies."

"We saw Tonnerre going off to the castle the other night," said Diana. "But the thing is, I can't picture him doing any acrobatics – climbing up walls and so on. He's so big."

Snubby remembered what Old Ma had told him. "He was a very good acrobat," he told the others. "And Old Ma says he can still walk tightropes and do things like that although he's so enormous."

"How do you suppose he goes through locked doors?" asked Diana.

"Perhaps he has skeleton keys, or whatever you call them," said Snubby. "Or perhaps he can wiggle the lock with a wire like some burglars can. Or perhaps . . ."

"It's all perhaps, perhaps," said Diana impatiently. "If only we could find out something solid. It's impossible to think of Tonnerre doing the robbery – and yet he went off to the castle the other night, and we know he's the one who decides where the fair's to go and it always seems to go to a place where there is a valuable collection of papers."

"It's a good old mystery," said Snubby. "And we're going to solve it. We've only got to hide somewhere in the grounds of the castle some time before midnight and watch who comes, and what he does. Easy!"

"Oh, very easy!" said Diana mockingly. "And how do you suppose you're going to get into the grounds? Can you walk through a locked gate or through a high wall?"

"It's easy enough to get into the grounds," said Barney. "There are spikes at the top of the wall. We can chuck up a rope-ladder, let it catch on the spikes, and climb up."

"Well, I'm not sitting on any spikes, thank you," said Diana promptly.

"Diana's not very helpful, is she?" said Snubby, getting annoyed with her. "Let's leave her out of it."

"No," said Barney. "She's in it all right. Of course she doesn't want to sit on spikes. Nobody does. But we'll just take half a dozen sacks, fold them, and pop them over the spikes. We can climb over easily enough then."

"And hide somewhere where we can watch the windows of that wing," said Snubby. "Gosh – we'll go tonight, won't we? All of us! What an adventure!"

"Yes – tonight," said Barney. "We'll meet at eleven o'clock, near the gate. And for goodness sake, keep quiet – just in case somebody else is hiding there too."

21

Midnight at the Castle

Snubby could hardly contain himself all day. He whistled and sang and was altogether so noisy and restless that Great-uncle Robert nearly went mad. Wherever he was he could hear Snubby making a noise. What was the matter with that boy?

The evening came at last. To Mrs Lynton's surprise, Snubby didn't seem to be hungry for his dinner. Nor Diana. Roger ate stolidly as usual. He wasn't so excitable as the other two.

"Do you feel quite well, Snubby?" asked Mrs Lynton anxiously when he refused a second helping. "And you too, Diana?"

"I'm all right," said Snubby, and Mrs Lynton, looking at his bright red cheeks and shining eyes, had no more doubts of his health.

"I suppose you've been stuffing yourself up with sweets and ice creams again," she said. "Well, I shall think twice about getting you a nice supper if you do that."

They all went to bed at the usual time but they didn't undress. Roger fell asleep and had to be woken up at half past ten.

"Are Mum and Dad in bed yet?" whispered Roger.

"Yes. They went early, thank goodness. There isn't a light anywhere except in Great-uncle's room," said Diana. "He's reading in bed, I expect."

They crept downstairs, warning each other to look out for Sardine. But Sardine was away on business of her own that night. Loony crept down with them, his tail-stump wagging. What was up?

They went into the moonlit garden, and out of the gate. Then they made off across the fields to Marloes Castle. There was a short cut to it which didn't take very long.

They came to the big iron gates, and then disappeared into the hedge on the other side. Diana gave a sudden little scream.

"Shut up, idiot!" Roger said fiercely in a low tone. Diana pulled away from him, shaking.

"There's somebody there already!" she whispered. "Oh, Roger!"

So there was. But it was only Barney and Miranda, who had got there first and happened to choose just the bit of hedge that Diana had pushed herself into! Barney came out grinning.

"Sorry I scared you, Diana. You scared

189

me too. You were all so quiet I didn't hear you. I got an awful fright when you pushed against me in the hedge."

"Have you seen anything or anyone?" asked Roger.

"Not a thing," said Barney. "Come on. We'll choose a place to get over the wall. I've got a rough rope-ladder and a few thick sacks. Carry the sacks, Roger and Snubby, and I'll take the rope."

With Miranda on his shoulder, and Loony at his heels, Barney led the way, keeping to the shadows of the hedge. They came at last to a place where the wall curved round, and the spikes did not seem to be quite so thick.

"This'll do," said Barney in a low voice. "Snubby, will Loony growl if he hears anyone, and warn us?"

"Yes, of course," said Snubby. "Loony, do you hear? You're on guard. On guard!"

"Woof," said Loony, understanding at once, and he sat down, ears, eyes and nose all on guard together.

The four of them got busy. Barney deftly threw the rope-ladder up to the spikes. The first time it slithered back again. The second time the spikes held one of the rungs. Barney pulled. It was quite tight. Up he went like a cat, his feet treading the wooden rungs lightly. "Chuck up the sacks," he whispered down. Roger and Snubby threw them up one by one.

Barney put them in a neat pile over a dozen or so of the sharp pointed spikes. Then, sitting on the sacks, he pulled at the rope-ladder till he had got a lot of loose slack up – enough to let half the ladder down the other side into the grounds!

"That's jolly clever!" thought Roger admiringly. "A ladder up to the top – and a ladder down the other side – and a pile of sack in the middle to protect him against the spikes! I should never have thought of all that."

"Come on up," whispered Barney.

Diana went up first. Barney helped her over and she sat on the sacks beside him. He then helped her down the other side. Then came Roger. Then Snubby, hauling up Loony with great difficulty, helped by Barney.

"No good leaving him outside the wall," gasped Snubby. "He'd bark the place down. Gosh, Loony, you're an awful lump. Whoa there – you're falling! I say, he's gone down the other side at top speed. He'll break his legs!"

There was a thud and a yelp. Diana called up softly: "It's all right. He's not hurt. He's like Sardine, always falls on his feet!"

Barney pulled up the ladder so that no one could climb up it from the road. The place he had chosen to climb over the wall was in deep shadow, and nobody could see the pile of sacks on the spikes from the road, Barney slipped down and joined the others.

"Where shall we hide?" whispered Roger, excited.

Barney stood a moment or two to get his bearings. "There are the barred windows up there," he whispered. "Let's make our way to that clump of trees. We can watch the windows easily from there."

They crept from tree to tree and shrub to shrub until they were under the clump that Barney had decided on. From there they could easily see the barred windows. Now, if any thief were going to enter from outside, they couldn't possibly help seeing him!

They found a dry place under a bush and huddled together, parting the branches to keep a good lookout on the windows. From somewhere not far off a church clock began to strike. It chimed first – and then deep clanging sounds came through the moonlit night.

"One, two, three," counted Snubby under his breath. "It's going to strike twelve. It's midnight! We must watch out. Lie down, Loony. Not a whimper from you! On guard, old fellow. On guard!"

There wasn't a sound anywhere. Not even an owl hooted. Then a nightingale began to sing. But it didn't sing for long – just tried out its notes and stopped. Not for a week or two would it sing all night long.

The children watched the moon move slowly across the sky, and waited patiently. Loony listened with both his ears. Diana always thought he would be able to hear much better if his ear-holes were not covered up by such long drooping ears. But, drooping ears or not, he still heard twice as well as they did.

The church clock chimed the quarter and then the half-hour. Snubby yawned. Diana felt cold. Miranda cuddled inside Barney's shirt and went to sleep.

The clock chimed the three-quarters. Still there was no sound. There was not even a tiny breeze blowing that night, and no mouse or rat or rabbit was to be seen or heard.

"I say – I don't think the thief's coming tonight," whispered Barney. "It's long past midnight. This can't be the night. We'd better go."

Nobody minded! They were cold and tired. The excitement had fizzled out and they all thought longingly of nice warm beds. Loony gave a sigh of relief when he felt them on the move once more.

"Come on, then," said Diana thankfully. "We've had enough for tonight. We'll try again tomorrow."

They made their way to the wall, still keeping well in the shadows, just in case anyone was about.

Over the wall they went and down the other side. Barney sat on the sacks beside the rope, unhitched it from the spikes, and threw it down to Roger.

"Have to leave the sacks here and hope no one notices them," he said, taking a flying leap to the ground. He landed on hands and knees and rolled over, quite unhurt. He sat up.

"Don't you think the sacks will be noticed by anyone coming down the lane?" asked Diana anxiously.

"No. This bit of the wall is well hidden by trees and, unless anyone is actually walking just below, looking up, I don't think they'd be noticed," said Barney. "We'll stuff the rope-ladder under this bush. Save us carrying it to and fro."

They were silent and disappointed as they went off down the lane. They said good-night at the fork, and Barney went one way and they another, taking the short cut across the fields.

"Better luck next time," said Roger to Diana rather gloomily, when he said good-night. "Gosh, I'm sleepy."

They all overslept the next morning, of course, and Mr Lynton told them wrathfully that they would have to go to bed an hour earlier that night.

But alas, when the evening came, Barney, Roger and Diana were all feeling ill! Diana and the two boys had gone over to see Barney at Rilloby Fair, and Roger had bought some sausage sandwiches. Snubby refused them, and bought himself some tomato sandwiches, of which he was very fond.

As he was the only one who didn't feel very sick that night, everyone felt that the sausage sandwiches must be to blame! Barney put Young Un in charge of the hoopla stall and staggered off to the caravan he shared with somebody else, feeling very ill. Roger and Diana got home somehow, and promptly collapsed in the hall, holding their stomachs and groaning.

Snubby rushed to tell Mrs Lynton. "It's the sausage sandwiches," he explained.

"There must have been something wrong with them. They feel awfully sick."

They were, poor things. Mrs Lynton got them into bed and dosed them well. Snubby looked in on them and was quite shocked to see them looking so green.

"Oh, I say – what about tonight?" he asked in a loud whisper. "Will you be able to go and watch?"

Roger groaned. "Of course not. I don't feel as if I shall ever be able to get up again."

Diana didn't even answer when he asked her. She felt really ill. Snubby tiptoed out with a most surprised Loony, and fell over Sardine on the stairs.

"Oh, Snubby – don't do that," said Mrs Lynton crossly, looking out of the lounge door. "Can't you possibly be quiet when people are feeling ill?"

"Well, I like that!" said Snubby indignantly. "How did I know Sardine was lying in wait for me? It's Sardine you want to nag at, not me."

"Now, Snubby, don't you talk to me like that," began Mrs Lynton, advancing on him. But Snubby fled.

What about tonight? Somebody ought to watch, surely? All right – Snubby would watch all alone!

22

A Night Out For Snubby

Snubby went to bed very early, for two reasons. One was that Mrs Lynton was worried about the other two, and was inclined to be very cross with Snubby. He thought it best to get out of her way. The other was that he had quite made up his mind to go and watch in the castle grounds by himself that night, and he wanted to get a little sleep before he went.

So he popped off to bed immediately after supper and took an alarm clock with him, set for a quarter past eleven. He put it under his pillow, wrapped in a scarf so that it would be heard only by him. He hoped Roger wouldn't hear it.

Roger was sound asleep, exhausted by his bouts of sickness. Snubby didn't undress. He just got into bed and shut his eyes. Immediately he was asleep, and slept peacefully till the alarm went off. Loony, who was on his bed, leaped up in fright, barking.

"Shut up, you silly, crazy idiot!" said

Snubby fiercely, and Loony shut up. Snubby lay and listened for a moment, after he had shut off the alarm. Had anyone heard?

Apparently not. Roger muttered something in his sleep, but that was all. Nobody else seemed to be stirring. Good! Snubby got cautiously out of bed and felt for his clothes, remembered with agreeable surprise that he was fully dressed, and got his jacket out of the cupboard. He had been cold the night before, and Snubby didn't like feeling cold!

"Come on, Loony – and if you fall over Sardine on the stairs I'll drown you," Snubby threatened. They got downstairs safely, and were soon running over the fields, Loony surprised but pleased at this second unusual excursion.

They came to the castle walls as the church clock struck the three-quarters. "A quarter to midnight," thought Snubby, feeling feverishly about in the bush for the rope-ladder. "Blow it – where's the ladder? Is this the right bush?"

It wasn't. Loony knew the right bush and dragged out the ladder for Snubby. Then followed an agonised five minutes with Snubby trying to throw the ladder up to the spikes.

It wasn't as easy as it had looked when Barney did it. Snubby grew extremely hot and agitated.

"Go up and stick, you beast of a ladder!"

he muttered. And miraculously, the ladder did stick on a spike or two, and held.

Up went Snubby joyfully, pleased to find that the ladder was fairly close to the pile of sacks that Barney had left on the spikes. He lifted them off and pulled them to the rope-ladder. Soon he was sitting on them, the spikes beneath him blunted by the sacking. He hauled up the ladder in the way that Barney had done, and soon half was on one side of the wall and half on the other. Snubby felt really proud of himself.

As he climbed down the other side, into the grounds, the church clock struck mid-night. *Dong, dong, dong*, it began. A whine reached Snubby, and he stopped short.

"Blow! I've forgotten Loony. I don't see how I'm going to get him up without help. He'll have to stay on the other side. I'll put him on guard."

He climbed up to the top again and whis-pered to Loony. "It's all right, old fellow, I shan't be long. You're on guard, see? On guard."

Loony settled down with a whimper. All right, he would be on guard – but he thought it was very mean of Snubby to go off without him.

Snubby crept over to the clump of trees where he and the others had stood the night before. It was a moonlit night again but with much more cloud about. There were periods of brilliant light and then periods of darkness when the moon went behind clouds. Snubby settled down under a bush and waited.

He felt extremely pleased with himself. He had been the only one sensible enough not to have the sausage sandwiches. He had actually got over the wall by himself – and he didn't feel a scrap scared. Not a scrap. He hadn't even got Loony with him and he felt as brave as a lion. Yes, Snubby felt very pleased with himself indeed, ready for anything that might happen.

The moon went in. Everywhere became dark – and in the darkness Snubby thought he heard a little noise. He didn't know if it was near him or not. He listened, and thought he heard another small noise. No, it wasn't near him – it was over by the castle, he thought. He waited impatiently for the moon to come out again.

When it came out Snubby got a terrific shock. A black shadow seemed to be climbing up the side of the castle walls! Up it went, and up, lithe and confident. Snubby strained his eyes. Who was it? It was too far away to see. Was it Tonnerre? No, surely it wasn't nearly big enough for him – but the moonlight played tricks with your eyes.

It looked as if the black figure was climbing up a pipe, leaping on to the window-sills, climbing up again – now scrambling up

ivy. This was the thief all right. No doubt
about that!

But how was he going to get through the
barred windows? Snubby held his breath to
see. The bars were too close together. Oh,
bother the moon – it had gone behind a
cloud again.

When it came sailing out once more there was no sign of the climbing figure. It had vanished. Snubby suddenly began to feel very scared indeed. His hair gradually rose up from his head with a horrid prickly sensation. Shivers went down his spine. He longed for Loony.

His eyes began to play tricks with him. Was that a figure standing at the bottom of the castle walls, far below the barred windows? Or was it a shadow? Was that a figure halfway up the walls? No, no, that was the outline of a small window. Was that a figure up on the roof by the chimney? No, no, of course not, it was a shadow, just the shadow of the chimney. And was that a . . .?

Snubby groaned and shut his eyes. He was scared stiff. Why had he come? Why had he thought he was so brave? He daren't look anywhere because he thought he saw sinister figures creeping, climbing, running. Oh, Loony, Loony, if only you weren't on the other side of the wall!

There was a noise near him. Somebody was panting not far off. Snubby turned quite cold with fear. He stayed absolutely still, hoping that whoever or whatever it was would go away.

But it didn't. It came nearer and nearer. There was the crack of twigs, the rustle of dead leaves under the bushes.

Snubby nearly died of fright.

And then, worse than ever, something stuck itself into his back and snuffled there. Snubby was absolutely petrified. What on earth was it?

A tiny whimper came to him, and Snubby felt so relieved that he could have wept. It was Loony!

He got the spaniel's head in his hands and let the delighted Loony lick his face till it was wet all over. "Loony!" he whispered. "It's really you! How did you get here? You couldn't climb that ladder! Oh, Loony, I was never so glad to see you in all my life!"

Loony was simply delighted at his welcome. Having been left on guard, he had been afraid that Snubby would be very angry to see him. But it was all right. Snubby was pleased, very, very pleased. It didn't matter that Loony had left the place he had to guard, had found a convenient hole by the wall, and had enlarged it to go underneath it with terrific squeezings and struggling.

Everything was all right. He had found his master, and what a welcome he had got!

Snubby recovered completely from his fright. He sat with his arm round Loony and squeezed him, telling him in whispers what he had seen. Then he stiffened again as Loony growled softly, his hackles rising at the back of his neck.

"What is it? What's the matter? Is it the

thief coming back?" whispered Snubby. But it was quite impossible to see anything because the moon was now behind a very big cloud indeed. Loony went on growling softly. Snubby didn't dare to move. He thought he heard noises from the direction of the castle and longed for the moon to come out again.

It came out for a fleeting instant and Snubby thought he saw a black figure descending the walls again, but he couldn't be sure. Anyway he was sure of one thing – he wasn't going to move from his hiding-place for a very long while! He didn't want to bump up against that terrifying robber.

He cuddled up to Loony, and put his head on the dog's warm, silky-coated body. Loony licked him lovingly.

Most surprisingly, Snubby went to sleep. When he awoke he couldn't at first think where he was. Then, with a twinge of fright, he remembered. Good gracious – how long had he been asleep? He waited till the church clock struck again, and found with relief that he hadn't slept for more than half an hour. How could he have gone to sleep like that? Anyway it should be safe to go home again now. Surely the thief would have gone long since. My word, what a tale he had to tell the others!

Feeling a good deal braver with Loony at his heels, Snubby pushed his way cautiously out of the bush. The moon came out and lit up the castle brilliantly. Nothing was to be seen of any climbing, creeping figure. With a sigh of relief, Snubby made his way to the wall.

Somehow he missed his way and wandered too far to the left, towards the iron gates. And then he got a really dreadful shock!

He came through a little copse of trees and found himself looking into a small dell – and from the dell many pairs of gleaming eyes looked up at him! He could see small shadowy bodies behind – but it was the eyes that frightened him. The moon sent its beams into the little dell and picked out the glassy, staring eyes that seemed to watch Snubby warily.

Loony growled and then barked, his hackles rising again. He backed away and began to whimper. Then Snubby knew that poor Loony too was scared, and he turned and fled. How he ran, stumbling through bushes and shrubs, tearing his jacket, scratching his hands, away, away from those gleaming eyes that waited for him in the dell.

How he found the ladder he never knew. He climbed up it, pulled it up behind him, loosened it from the spikes and sent it down to the ground. He left the sacks and flung himself to the ground. He wasn't as clever as Barney at this kind of thing, and fell far too heavily, twisting one ankle and bruising his knees badly.

Loony ran to find his hole. He squeezed through with difficulty and raced up to Snubby. Snubby was trembling, almost in tears. He flung his arms round Loony's neck.

"Stay with me, Loony. Let's go home. There's something strange about and I don't like it. Keep near me."

Loony had every intention of doing so. He wasn't feeling too happy himself. He kept as close to Snubby's feet as he could, almost tripping him up at times. The two of them took the short cut across the fields and got home at last.

Roger was sound asleep. So was Diana. Snubby longed to wake them up and tell them everything, but he hadn't the heart to. They had both been so very, very sick.

But he woke them up early in the morning and told them! He shook Roger and woke up Diana. He made Roger go into Diana's room, and then he told them both.

"I had an adventure last night," he said. "You'll never believe it. Listen!"

23

It's All in the Papers!

Roger and Diana still felt a little weak from their upset of the day before. They were not too pleased at being awakened so early. But they soon pricked up their ears when they heard Snubby's story.

He exaggerated, of course, which was a pity. He related how he had gone to the wall and got over it, how he had waited without Loony, and how he had suddenly seen the black figure climbing up the wall.

"Up and up," said Snubby, "jumping from windowsill to windowsill, climbing up the ivy, using pipes – gosh, you should have seen him. Talk about an acrobat!"

"Was it Tonnerre?" asked Roger excitedly.

"Might have been," said Snubby. "I was too far away to see. And there was a figure at the foot of the walls too – and one on the roof – and . . ."

By the time Snubby had finished it sounded as if the castle grounds had been swarming with thieves!

"I saw something else too," went on Snubby. "Both of us saw them, Loony too. And Loony was really scared."

"I bet you were too," said Diana.

"I was as brave as could be!" said Snubby most untruthfully, having completely forgotten his terror. "Do listen. Well, we came to a little kind of dell – and there lying in wait for us were all kinds of things with gleaming eyes!"

"And I suppose you did what any sensible person would have done – you took to your heels and fled?" said Roger.

"Well, I didn't stay long," admitted Snubby. "Nor would you."

"You bet I wouldn't!" said Roger. "What did they do? Snarl? Growl? Call out?"

"Oh – a kind of mixture of all the lot," said Snubby, exaggerating wildly again. "And one or two took a step forward as if they were going for Loony and me."

Diana and Roger couldn't help being impressed by all this. "Could you take us to see this field?" asked Roger.

"In the daytime, not at night," said Snubby promptly. "We'll go this morning."

But they didn't. When Snubby got down to breakfast, late as usual, but forgiven because he offered to take up breakfast trays to Roger and Diana, he found everyone exclaiming over the morning paper.

"What's up?" asked Snubby, and suddenly

he knew. Of course – the robbery! It would be in the paper!

So it was – with big headlines.

STRANGE ROBBERY LAST NIGHT AT MARLOES CASTLE
STUFFED ANIMALS TAKEN
AND LEFT IN GROUNDS
IS THIEF A MADMAN?
HOW DID HE GET THROUGH FASTENED WINDOWS AND LOCKED DOORS?

Snubby looked over the shoulders of the grown-ups and read the report. There it all was. Somebody had mysteriously got into the locked room and had taken – how strange – taken all the smaller animals, but apparently nothing else!

Snubby felt himself blushing. Those gleaming eyes – they must have been the eyes of the stuffed animals that the thief had put together in that little dell. Why had he said anything about the creatures making noises and moving towards him? Oh gosh, the others would tease him like anything!

Snubby ate his breakfast very soberly. He didn't say a word about what he knew. He would let the grown-ups discuss it, and wondered what to say to Roger and Diana upstairs. He was very puzzled. Why had the thief taken worthless animals? Why hadn't he stolen the valuable papers there? It didn't make sense. Was the thief really a madman? Then he must be a different thief from the one that so sensibly took rare papers!

And anyway how did even a madman get into that room? Snubby had seen him climbing the wall – but according to the papers the windows were still fastened and the bars unbroken.

Great-uncle Robert suddenly gave a loud exclamation and made everyone jump.

"Listen to this. It's in the stop-press news. They've found a clue to the thief."

"What?" Mr and Mrs Lynton and Snubby chorused.

Great-uncle Robert lowered the paper and spoke in a very peculiar kind of voice.

"The clue they've found, out in the grounds, is – a *green glove*!"

He stared hard at Snubby. Snubby went pale. Gosh – how extraordinary. Why ever had he made up that silly story of the Green Hands Gang that wore green gloves. It was going to haunt him for the rest of his life.

"I think," said Great-uncle ominously, "I think it must be the Green Hands Gang. What do you think, Snubby?"

Mr and Mrs Lynton stared at Great-uncle and Snubby in bewilderment. Snubby swallowed down his last bit of toast, nearly choked, and got up.

"I – er – I don't know anything about a Green Hands Gang," he said. "Nothing at

all. Aunt Susan, I'll go and get Roger's tray, and Diana's."

Mr Lynton turned to Great-uncle when Snubby had gone. "What is all this?" he said. "It sounds like a film plot or something – Green Hands Gang! Absurd!"

"The time has come for me to tell you what I know," said Great-uncle solemnly. "It isn't much. I dismissed it, the last few days, as something silly that Snubby made up – but now that a green glove has been found, things look different."

Whereupon he told them the fairytale that Snubby had told him in the train, about the gang that had its hold on Snubby because of his stumbling on their plot, his running away, and how he had told Great-uncle that the gang, called the Green Hands Gang because they wore green gloves, would be operating at Ricklesham – stealing valuable papers.

"And bless us all, so they did," said Uncle Robert. "And here's a theft again – and a green glove is dropped!"

"Snubby's been pulling your leg, Uncle Robert," said Mrs Lynton soothingly. "I'll speak to him about this."

"Yes – but the green glove!" said Uncle Robert. "The boy couldn't have made that up. There actually is a clue of a green glove."

"Coincidence – sheer chance," said Mr Lynton impatiently. "Snubby doesn't know a thing. He needs a serious punishment and I'll see he gets it."

"No, no – don't do that," said Uncle Robert in alarm. "I really do think Snubby knows something. Give him a chance, Richard. I wouldn't have given him away if I'd known you would punish him."

"Oh, it's been coming to him for some long time," said Mr Lynton, gathering up his letters. "You can tell him from me that he's going to get punished – unless, of course he really does know something and can produce a member of this wonderful gang who actually does wear green gloves. Pah!"

Out he went. Great-uncle Robert sighed. He was getting mixed up in a lot of things. Dear, dear – to think Marloes Castle was burgled and not one of those precious papers taken – only the stuffed animals. Extraordinary!

Snubby tiptoed into the room where only Great-uncle was left there.

"What did you tell them?" he demanded. "Uncle Richard's furious. I can tell by the way he went out."

"My boy, I told them what you had told me and they not only disbelieved your whole tale – in spite of the green gloves," said Great-uncle solemnly, "but your uncle, I very much regret to say, is going to punish you – unless you can – er – produce one of the green glove thieves."

"You shouldn't have given me away," said poor Snubby, feeling very sorry for himself indeed. "Didn't I twist my ankle last night, and bruise my knees – look – and now I'm to be punished. It isn't fair. Especially as I know more than anyone else about the burglary!"

"Do you?" said Great-uncle, startled. "Or is that just another of your tales?" he asked more cautiously. "Tell me."

"I'm not telling you or anybody else a single thing," declared Snubby, almost in tears. "Sneaking and blabbing like that! Getting me punished. It's not fair. I wish there was a Green Hands Gang – I'd jolly well set them on to everyone in this house, and be glad to!"

He went out and slammed the door. Great-uncle was upset and worried. He also felt extremely muddled. Dear, dear, Snubby was a most unreliable and really extraordinary boy!

24

The Police Arrive

Suddenly quite a lot of things began to happen. The first one was the arrival of the police!

"I say – there's Inspector Williams coming up the front path and somebody in plain clothes with him – a detective, I should think!" called Roger in excitement.

"Why should they come here?" said Diana. Snubby began to shake at the knees. Had Great-uncle said anything to the police about the Green Hands Gang? Surely not!

Poor Snubby crept into the boxroom and shut the door. He was absolutely certain that the police had come to question him about his idiotic Green Hands story.

"I'll never make up a tale again, never," vowed poor Snubby. "This one has followed me and followed me – and however much I say I made it up, no one will believe me now that a green glove has been found."

The Inspector asked for Great-uncle Robert. He and his colleague were shown into the study. "Mr Robert Grey?" asked the Inspector. "I've come in connection with this peculiar Marloes Castle case, sir. Lord Marloes asked us to come and have a word with you. He is thinking of placing all his papers somewhere in safety now that a thief has actually been able to get into the room where he keeps them. Funny business that, sir – taking the animals and leaving the papers. Must be mad, I should think."

"Very strange indeed," agreed Great-uncle. "Er – does Lord Marloes want me to do anything about the papers for him?"

"Yes, sir. He wondered if you would go up to the castle and advise the custodian how to pack them, and in what order they should be packed, and so on," said the Inspector.

"I'd be pleased to," said Great-uncle.

"There's another thing," said the Inspector. "When you went there with the children the other day, sir, did you notice two other men there?"

"Yes, I did," said Great-uncle. "Why?"

"Well, sir, anyone visiting the Marloes Collection has to have a pass on which is written his name and address," said the Inspector. He gave Great-uncle three passes. "That's yours, sir, with the names of the three children on. That's another visitor's, a Professor Cummings, a very, very bent old fellow. And here's another – name of Alfred

James Smith, address given as 38 Thurlow Crescent, Leeds. Well, we've checked yours, of course, and Professor Cummings – addresses given, correct. But in the case of this third one, sir . . ."

"It's false, I suppose?" said Great-uncle Robert, getting excited. "But why? And what's the connection between a man with a false name and address coming to look at the papers, and another man, presumably mad, coming to steal the stuffed animals. It doesn't make sense."

"You're right, it doesn't," agreed the Inspector, and the plain-clothes man nodded his head. "But it may be there is a connection, and we want to find out all we can about this fellow with the false name and address. Can you give us an exact description, sir?"

"Well, no, I can't. I hardly noticed him," said Great-uncle. "But why not ask the three children? They're as sharp as needles, all of them. They'll give you a full description."

"Good idea. Can you get them for us, sir?" said the Inspector. Great-uncle rose and went out. He called loudly.

"Roger! The police want to have a word with you three. Come down, will you?"

Roger felt excited. What was up? He went to fetch Diana. "Where's Snubby? Snubby! I say, Snubby! Where are you? The police want to talk to you."

Snubby's heart went cold inside him. He clutched at the trunk he was sitting on. Now what would happen to him?

"Snubby! Where are you?" yelled Roger. He opened the boxroom door. "Gosh, what do you think you're doing in here, all alone with Loony? Didn't you hear me calling you? Come on down. The police want a word with us."

Snubby rose and with shaking knees went down the stairs. Roger and Diana rushed down, excited.

"Good morning, youngsters," said the Inspector with a very nice smile. "I want a word with you. Now, did any of you notice the two men who were in the room with you at Marloes Castle, when you went to see the animals and the papers?"

Snubby's heart lightened a little. Perhaps the police hadn't come for him after all.

Roger nodded. "Yes, I remember them quite well. One was very old and bent – he bent so far forward that we couldn't see his face."

"And the other one was so hairy you couldn't see his face either!" said Diana.

The plain-clothes man, who had been writing in a little notebook, looked up at this description.

"How hairy was he?" he asked.

"Well," said Diana, "he had very thick hair on his head, thick shaggy eyebrows, a thick moustache and a beard. You couldn't tell what he was really like at all, because he was all hair!"

"Was he big?" asked the detective.

"Yes," said Diana, "a heavy sort of man. Why, do you know him?"

The detective was turning back some pages of his note-book. "Your description happens to fit men who were known to visit two collections of rare documents, some of which were stolen recently," he said. "It fits exactly, in fact."

The children digested this in silence.

"Then do you think that's the man that stole the other papers – and stole the animals from Marloes Castle too?" asked Roger at last. "Why should he take those moth-eaten animals?"

"Ask me another!" said the detective. "Now – would you know this hairy man again if you saw him?"

"Yes – if he was still hairy," said Roger. "But I should think most of the hair was false!"

"You're probably right," said the Inspector. "Er – did you see the man's hands, by any chance?"

The children frowned, trying to remember. "I saw him using a magnifying glass, sliding it up and down the pages," said Roger. "And as far as I can remember he had quite ordinary hands – I didn't notice that they were very hairy, now I come to think of it, and perhaps they should have been as he was such a hairy man. Great-uncle Robert's got an awful lot of hair and his hands are hairy on the back – look."

Everyone gazed at Great-uncle's hairy hands. He looked rather uncomfortable, and put them in his pockets as soon as he could.

"Would you say that the hairy man could wear this glove?" said the Inspector, producing a green glove from his pocket.

The children gazed at the glove. Loony went over to it and sniffed it excitedly. He pawed at it and whined.

"Why – he knows who wore that glove!" said Snubby, astonished. "That's the way he always acts if you show him anything that smells of a person he knows."

"Aha – now we're getting somewhere!" said the detective, sitting up suddenly. "You sure your dog knows the owner of that glove? Quite sure? Then that narrows things down considerably. The owner of the glove must be somebody you children know."

"Gosh!" said Roger, his thoughts flying to Tonnerre at once. He looked closely at the glove. It was a small one, made of the very softest, finest leather imaginable. No – he didn't think it would fit Tonnerre. As far as he remembered, Tonnerre had very large hands – or had he? Perhaps he hadn't, perhaps Roger only thought that because Tonnerre was enormous and therefore it seemed right for him to have large hands.

Snubby took the glove and looked at it. Loony stood on his hind legs, still sniffing and whining. If only he could speak – what name would he say?

"Who wears this glove, Loony?" asked Snubby.

"Woof!" said Loony at once. The detective took the glove from Snubby and tossed it to the Inspector. He didn't want Loony to nibble their biggest clue.

"You haven't answered my question," said the Inspector, pocketing the glove. "I asked you if you thought the hairy man could have worn a glove as small as this."

The children thought hard.

"Yes, he might," said Roger.

"I don't remember," said Diana.

"He couldn't possibly," said Snubby.

"Hmm – very helpful!" said the Inspector with a laugh. "Well thanks, children. That's all I want to ask you. Keep your eyes open for the hairy man, will you? It's just possible he might tell us a few interesting things if we can find him."

Snubby escaped thankfully, throwing a grateful glance at Great-uncle Robert.

Loony tore after the children. Roger stopped to pat him. "So you know who the owner of the green glove is, do you?" he said. "Who wore that glove so as not to leave fingerprints, Loony? And where's the other glove of the pair? Can't you find it? Can't you tell us anything?"

"Woof-woof!" said Loony joyfully, enjoying this earnest conversation, and leaping round Roger excitedly.

"It's funny about that hairy man, isn't it?" said Diana. "What was he doing there that day, if he was the thief? Looking to see if there were any papers worth stealing – or what?"

"Goodness knows," said Roger. "It's all a muddle – the hairy man – the green glove – the stolen animals – and Loony knowing who it is! It's really very, very peculiar."

25

Quite a Lot of Talk!

Roger and Diana felt quite themselves again, and suggested going over to see Barney to find out if he had got over his attack of sickness too. They had a tremendous lot to tell him!

"Yes, you go and see him," said Mrs Lynton. "A walk on this sunny morning will do you good after that nasty attack you had yesterday. Be careful what you buy at the fair this time, please. You'd be wise not to buy any food there at all, after your horrid experience."

They went off together, Loony wild with delight at the thought of a walk. He capered ahead, putting his head down every hole they came to, sniffing for rabbits.

Barney was quite all right again. He had felt very sick and ill all night, but had at last gone to sleep and slept soundly till ten o'clock that morning. Now he was up and about, whistling, giving his hoopla stall a really good clean down.

"It's Saturday," he explained. "We always get most people that day, so I like to have everything looking spick and span. Hey, Miranda, leave Loony alone. If you pull his long ears, he'll pull your long tail!"

But that's just what Loony couldn't do because Miranda aggravatingly went and sat up on top of the round roof of the stall, swinging her tail well out of poor Loony's reach!

"Barney – have you seen the paper?" said Roger urgently.

"No," said Barney, surprised. "What's up? Gosh – you don't mean to say there's been a robbery at the castle! Blast! We've missed it. We were ill and didn't go to watch."

"Sh!" said Diana warningly. "We've heaps to tell you, Barney. Can you come into some safe place for half an hour where no one can hear us?"

"Let me finish cleaning my stall and I'll come," said Barney, looking thrilled. "I'll be another ten minutes. Go and talk to the chimps. They seem rather down in the mouth this morning." So they were. They sat together, their arms twined round one another, looking very mournful. "Have they had sausage sandwiches too?" Snubby asked Vosta. But Vosta seemed cross and answered him shortly.

"Don't be silly. I'd never give them that kind of food. They're all right. Tonnerre's

224

been at them, that's all. They can't bear his shouting."

"Nor can I," said Roger, putting his hand to his ears. He could hear Tonnerre yelling loudly. Somebody else was getting into trouble too. It was Young Un. He came along looking miserable.

"Shouted at me for nothing," he said to the children. "Said I'd kept some of his elephant-ride money for myself. I didn't. But I will next time."

"No, you mustn't," said Diana, shocked.

"Why not?" asked poor Young Un. "Look, he's told me off for something I didn't do. All right, I'll go and do it then, to earn my telling off. I'll be straight with him then."

"Straight with him and crooked with yourself," said Roger. "Don't do anything wrong, Young Un. You'll be sorry."

Young Un didn't think so. He'd get even with Tonnerre, see if he wouldn't. He went off muttering.

The children left the bad-tempered Vosta, and his mournful chimps with their arms still round one another, and went to see if Barney was ready. He was.

They went off to the caravan Barney shared with another boy. "We'll be all right here, if we talk quietly," said Barney. "Now, what's in the paper? What's happened?"

They had bought a paper on the way and

they showed it to Barney. His face was a picture as he read about the curious robbery. "Stuffed animals! Are they valuable?" he asked.

"Not these," said Roger. "They're the ones we saw ourselves, up in the castle – moth-eaten, badly-stuffed things."

"And I saw them in the castle grounds last night, where the thief had put them – and where the police found them this morning," put in Snubby. Barney's eyes nearly fell out of his head.

"What?" he said. "Did you go last night? All by yourself, to watch? My, but you're a brave one!"

Snubby swelled with pride at this. He told his story to Barney, who listened with intense interest.

"Barney, do you know anyone who wears green gloves – small ones?" asked Diana eagerly. "Especially an acrobatic man – one who could climb up steep walls and jump from sill to sill and all that?"

"Does Tonnerre wear green gloves ever?" asked Snubby in a whisper.

"Never seen him wear any gloves at all. Never seen anyone in the fair wear gloves," said Barney. "Why, they'd laugh at it!"

"Is there anyone in the fair who's an acrobat and has small hands?" asked Diana. "Anyone at all?"

Barney thought hard. "There's Vosta," he

said at last. "He's a fine acrobat, you know, though training chimps is his job here. And he's got small hands, almost like a woman's."

Vosta! Could it be Vosta?

"Did the figure you saw climbing up the wall look anything like Vosta?" Roger asked Snubby. Snubby considered.

"Well – it's difficult to say, because I really couldn't see him clearly. All I know is he seemed absolutely certain and confident in all his movements," said Snubby. "As if he was quite used to such amazing climbing and leaping."

"It can't be Vosta," said Barney. "He wouldn't be such an idiot as to steal the wrong things. The one who steals the papers and things must either know them himself or be told in great detail which to take. Vosta wouldn't be such an idiot. Something went wrong last night."

Roger got out his map – the map he had made of the room in the castle.

"We mustn't forget that once again the thief apparently got in through fastened and locked windows," he said. "The paper says he didn't go through the locked doors because there's a burglar alarm set there, which rings if a door is opened at night. And the alarm didn't ring, so the doors weren't opened."

They looked at the map, poring over it. It

was obvious that the thief meant to get in through the windows, as he climbed the outside walls. But how did he unfasten windows that were locked on the inside? And how in the world did he squeeze through the narrow bars?

"Give it up!" said Roger. "Unless by any chance he was Santa Claus and came down the chimney! Now that's an idea – would the thief be Santa Claus, do you suppose? Snubby, did it look like Santa climbing up the walls?"

"Don't be daft," said Snubby. "All the same – I did think I saw a figure up on the roof, by the chimney."

"You saw figures everywhere, according to you," said Diana disbelievingly. "The trouble with you, Snubby, is that we never know how much you are exaggerating."

"You don't suppose the thief could come down the chimney, do you?" asked Roger suddenly. "Joking apart, I mean. Look, I've marked where the fireplace is in this map. There was only one chimney up on the roof of that wing, because I expect all the fireplaces in the wing are under one another, in each room, and one chimney serves for all."

"These old houses have very wide chimneys," said Diana. "Big enough for a man to come down them quite easily, I should think."

"That fireplace didn't look awfully big,

though," said Snubby, remembering. "I could have got down, perhaps – but I'm pretty certain that a fellow as big as Tonnerre couldn't."

"Then we'll have to rule the chimney out too," said Roger. "It's strange, you know. It's impossible for anyone to have gone through the burglar-alarmed doors – it's impossible for anyone to have unfastened the windows from outside – and we're agreed that the chimney and fireplace are too small for anyone to get down those. All these impossibilities – and yet somebody found it possible to enter that room, and take from it a dozen or so stuffed animals!"

"He couldn't have taken them all at once," said Snubby. "There were too many. He must have made a good many journeys. I suppose he did all his climbing up and down while I popped off to sleep for half an hour."

"Well! You didn't tell us that before!" said Diana.

"I didn't think about it," said Snubby.

Footsteps came up the caravan steps at that moment and the door was flung open. Tonnerre stood there, black as thunder.

"So! This is where you idle with your fine friends, Barney!" he roared. "Reading the newspapers, too, when you should be doing your work!"

He snatched the paper from Barney and

tore it across. Snubby began to tremble. He really was scared of Tonnerre.

"Get back to your work," he roared to Barney. "And you! You clear out of my field!" he shouted at the others. "Not this boy, though. Aha, it is the little snooper again. I will take him to my caravan and teach him a few things. Come, my little snooper."

Poor Snubby was hauled off before the others could do anything. Roger and Barney ran off after the angry Tonnerre, but they might as well have been dogs barking at a bull for all the notice he took of them. He really was in a towering rage!

Barney ran to Old Ma. "Old Ma – can you go after Mr Tonnerre and make him let Snubby go? He hasn't done anything."

But even Old Ma was afraid of Tonnerre that day. "A black-hearted man he is," she said, staring after him as he dragged poor Snubby to his caravan. "I can't do nothing with him in one of his black moods."

But Loony wasn't afraid of anyone if they were hurting his beloved Snubby. He flew at Tonnerre, snapping and growling. He snapped at his ankles all the way up the steps of Tonnerre's caravan, he tore his trousers as he went in, and he bit his leg so hard, at last, that Tonnerre dropped Snubby with a yell and turned on the dog.

Loony shot out of his way under the

bunk-beds. Snubby took his chance and leaped down the caravan steps, taking them all in one bound. Tonnerre leaped after him, also taking the steps in one bound.

Loony was scrabbling under the bunk. He came out with something in his mouth, and shot down the steps with it. He dropped it on the ground and went after Tonnerre again at top speed.

Diana, standing nearby, quite petrified by all this, looked to see what Loony had dropped. She stared in utter amazement.

It was a green glove – a partner to the one that the police had shown the children that morning!

26

The Second Green Glove

Diana picked up the glove at once. She stuffed it into the pocket of her jeans. She didn't know why she did that – she just felt that it was important that she should.

Snubby was now outside the field gate. Loony was worrying Tonnerre's ankles, and the giant-like man was kicking out at him, shouting. All the people in the fairground were watching, most of them silent.

Barney sidled up to Roger. "Get Diana and go. Go through the gate at the opposite end of the field. Snubby's all right now – he'll race home. Don't come back here. I shall leave this fair today. Tonnerre's got his knife into me, and I won't work for him any more. I'll come to your home and tell you what's happened as soon as I can. Go quickly now."

"Will you be all right, Barney?" asked Diana anxiously, as Roger pulled her away to the gate Barney had pointed to.

Barney nodded. "I know how to look

after myself. Tonnerre's had some bad luck – something's gone wrong. He's always like this then – a dangerous fellow. Did you notice his hands? Enormous! He couldn't have worn that green glove!"

Diana had no time to tell him about the other glove. She was being dragged out of the gate at top speed by Roger. They set off to skirt the field, and join poor Snubby.

They found him sitting on a fence by the roadside with Loony licking his ankles. He looked rather pale, and gave them a watery grin.

"Hello," he said. "So you escaped all right. Gosh – I'm scared stiff of Tonnerre. I shall dream about him all night."

"Come on home, quick. I've got something to show you," said Diana.

They went home together, Loony at their heels, occasionally looking back to see if Tonnerre was by any chance stalking them. But he wasn't, of course. He was probably giving poor Barney a bad time now!

Diana could hardly contain herself. She was bursting to produce the glove! "Come into the summerhouse quickly," she said. "Come on!"

They all went in and sat down. Sardine strolled in to join them. Loony wagged his tail, feeling so pleased with himself for biting Tonnerre that he couldn't even find it in him to chase Sardine.

Diana put her hand in her pocket and took out the green glove. The boys stared at it.

"Where did you get it?" asked Roger. "Did the police leave it somewhere?"

"No – it's not the glove they brought. It's the other glove!" said Diana. "What do you think of that?"

Roger snatched it up with a loud exclamation. "Good gracious! Where did you get it?"

"I didn't get it," said Diana. "Loony did. When Tonnerre took Snubby into his caravan, Loony followed, snapping and snarling. And when he came out he had this green glove in his mouth! He must have picked it up from the floor of the caravan."

Both boys stared at the glove, and Roger fingered it and turned it over in his hands. "What exactly does that mean, then?" he said. "As far as I can see, it means that although Tonnerre himself can't wear these, he lends them to someone who does – in other words, he lends them to the thief!"

"That's right," said Snubby. He bent down and held the glove to Loony's nose. The spaniel at once whined and sniffed excitedly.

"See? He knows the owner of this glove too – it's the same owner as the glove he sniffed this morning. It's somebody at the fair," said Snubby.

"It's Vosta then," said Roger. "I noticed he had quite small hands this morning."

Diana slipped the glove on to her own hand. It fitted her perfectly. She laughed. She put on a mysterious, sinister voice.

"I belong to the Green Hands Gang," she said in a deep, hollow voice. "See my green glove!"

Great-uncle Robert was coming up to the summerhouse with a book when he suddenly heard these words spoken in a very peculiar voice indeed. He stopped, alarmed.

Who was that speaking? What an extraordinary voice! And good gracious, was that a green-gloved hand appearing out of the door of the summerhouse?

It was. Diana was now doing a weird dance in the summerhouse, and waving her green-gloved hand about.

Great-uncle Robert was very surprised indeed. He suddenly walked determinedly up to the summerhouse and looked in, expecting to see something extraordinary.

All he saw was the three children and Loony, very startled by his sudden appearance. Diana put her green-gloved hand behind her back at once.

"What is the meaning of this?" Great-uncle asked irritably. "Diana, where did you get that glove? Tell me at once."

There was silence. Diana glanced desperately at the boys.

"Well?" said Great-uncle in quite a nasty voice. "Are you going to tell me or would you rather I called your parents? Diana, I am quite sure you children know something that we ought to know – that maybe even the police ought to know."

"We'd better tell him," said Roger to the others. "Anyway, I think it's got a bit beyond us now we've found this glove. All right, Great-uncle, we'll tell you all we know – and really, it's quite a lot."

"But first you'll have to believe that Snubby's tale of the Green Hands Gang was all a lot of nonsense," said Diana. "Or else you'll get muddled. It's just by chance that a pair of green gloves has come into this."

"Will you please begin to tell me all you know," said Great-uncle impatiently, and sat himself down on the wooden seat in the summerhouse.

Roger began the tale. Diana and Snubby added bits to it that he forgot. It was a long tale and an extraordinary one, especially the bit where Snubby had come across the gleaming-eyed creatures in the dell the night before. Great-uncle grunted.

"Hmm. An alarming experience. I hope it taught you a lesson! Tut-tut! What a story! And now what about this glove? It seems to me that this fellow Tonnerre had better be handed over to the police for questioning."

Snubby thought that was an awfully good

idea. Aha! He'd get a bit of his own back on Tonnerre then! Yes, Snubby certainly thought that was a very good idea.

"Give me the glove," said Great-uncle importantly. "And understand this — the matter is out of your hands entirely now. You've nothing to do with it, and you must keep your noses out of it or you'll get into trouble. This is for grown-ups to solve, not children."

But alas, not even Great-uncle, or Mr and Mrs Lynton, or even the police, seemed to be able to solve the mystery of Rilloby Fair and the thefts at the castle.

Mr Tonnerre said he didn't know anything at all about the green glove. Somebody must have put it into his caravan. He had never, never seen it before. Why should he have a green glove so small? See his enormous hands! It would fit his thumb and no more.

"Did you lend them to the thief to wear, in order that he might leave no fingerprints?" asked the Inspector patiently for the twentieth time. But Tonnerre shook his great head impatiently.

"What have I to do with thieves who steal stuffed animals? I, who have live ones of my own. I tell you, I know nothing of this pest of a green glove. Nothing at all."

And so the police had to let him go, because they certainly could not prove that

he had lent the gloves to anyone, or that he even knew the thief. He went back to his caravan grumbling loudly, and everyone kept well out of his way.

Then the police called on Vosta. What did he know about the gloves? Were they his? Had he ever worn them? Could he climb walls? Would he please put them on?

He did so – and certainly they seemed rather small for him, although his hands were not very large for a man.

The two chimpanzees watched the policemen when they went to Vosta's tent to interview him. They still seemed rather subdued, especially Burly, and sat quietly with their arms round one another's necks.

They were interested to see the gloves. They got up and peered at them and patted them.

239

"Anything new interests them," said Vosta, pushing the chimps away. "Go and sit down, you two. Look out for your hand-kerchief, Inspector, if you've got one in your pocket. They'll be after it, especially Hurly, who's a real pickpocket."

It was impossible to get anything helpful out of Vosta at all.

He just said he didn't know; he didn't know whose the gloves were, he didn't know who the thief was, he didn't know anything.

The Inspector put the gloves into his pocket impatiently. He felt that both Tonnerre and Vosta did know something – but he was up against a blank wall. He could ask no more questions, go no further.

He went off with the detective. Vosta made a grimace after them. He watched them go all the way across the field.

He didn't see Hurly show Burly something. He didn't see Burly hold out his paw for it. He didn't see the chimps tuck their find under the blankets in their bunk.

Hurly had picked the Inspector's pocket as he turned to go. He had got the pair of green gloves and now they were well hidden under the blankets!

The gloves excited Burly. He wanted to put them on. He must wait till Vosta wasn't there, because Vosta would take them away.

27

Sunday – and Monday

The next day came. It was Sunday. It seemed very peaceful and quiet after all the excitement of the day before.

Barney turned up in the morning with Miranda. He saw Roger at the window and waved. Roger open the window and shouted to him. "The others are in the summerhouse. I'm just coming."

Barney went to the summerhouse, and found Diana and Snubby there with Loony. Lonny gave Barney and Miranda a tremendous welcome.

"I say!" said Barney, looking at Diana in awe. "You going to a party or something? You're all dressed up. And Snubby looks awfully clean."

"No, we're not going to a party," said Diana, surprised. "It's Sunday, and we've just been to church, that's all. Don't you ever go?"

"No. But I'd like to," said Barney. He wanted to do everything these friends of his did, if he could. "Hello, Roger!"

Roger walked in, also looking very clean and spruce. "Hello, Barney," he said. "Have you left the fair?"

"No. Tonnerre won't let me go till the fair leaves Rilloby," said Barney. "But he's better now. Not nearly so fierce. I really think the visit of the police gave him a fright. I came to see if you'd got any more news. Solved the mystery yet?"

"No. I don't think it ever will be solved," said Roger. "It's just a list of impossible things – things that can't happen and yet did – with a pair of green gloves complicating everything still more."

"Listen," said Barney. "I shan't be able to see you tomorrow. Vosta's having the day off, goodness knows why – and I'm to see to the chimps. Young Un is taking the hoopla stall. You mustn't come to the fair again, of course. You'd be like a red rag to a bull if Tonnerre caught sight of you."

"Well, can't you spend the day with us today?" said Diana at once. "The fair doesn't open on Sundays. Wouldn't you like to be with us?"

"Well, yes, of course I would," said Barney, his blue eyes shining. "I love your home. But would your mother mind? And what about your father? He's home today, isn't he?"

"They won't mind if we keep out of their

242

way," said Diana. "They do like us to be quiet on Sundays, of course. But we can always talk and read."

"You lend me another of Shakespeare's plays," said Barney. "I'll be quiet enough then!"

The others laughed. It always amused them to see Barney labouring through a play by Shakespeare – determined to understand it, so that if ever he did come across his unknown father who had once acted in so many of Shakespeare's plays, he would at least have something in common with him.

"I'll lend you *Hamlet*," said Roger. "You'll like that, there's a super ghost in it."

Mrs Lynton was very willing for Barney to spend the day. Great-uncle Robert was not too pleased to see yet another child, complete with monkey, added to the riotous trio.

"How I'm ever going to get my Memoirs written, I don't know," he complained to Mrs Lynton. "Children and dogs and cats and monkeys everywhere I go!"

"You go and have your little nap in the study and I'll send the children outside on this wonderful day," said Mrs Lynton.

"I said 'my Memoirs', not a nap," said Great-uncle with dignity, and retired to the study. He carefully put out paper, fountain pen and notes on the table, headed a page "Chapter Five", and then promptly settled down in an armchair and went to sleep.

"Now don't you dare to disturb your Great-uncle," Mrs Lynton warned the children. "Don't let Miranda leap in at the window on to him – and don't let Loony bark – and see that Sardine doesn't get into the study and jump up on Great-uncle's knee."

"Right, Mum," said Roger. "And I'll tell that loud-voiced thrush to pipe down, and shoo all the bees out of the garden, and as for that earwig I saw stamping about this morning, I'll . . ."

"Now, now, Roger!" said his mother, smiling. "Don't be ridiculous. Go along to the summerhouse and don't let me hear a sound from any of you!"

Sunday was very peaceful. Barney enjoyed it more than anyone. It was heaven to him to be in a family, in a home, to belong, even for only one day, to a little company of people who liked him and accepted him as one of themselves.

"They can't understand what it's like not to have any people of your own, not to have a home you can always go to – no, not even Snubby understands, although he's got no parents. He belongs here. I don't belong anywhere," thought Barney soberly. "Perhaps if I ever find my father, I shall have a home with him, and belong there."

The children talked a lot about the green gloves, Tonnerre, Vosta, the castle and the rest. They went over and over everything again and again. What a mystery!

"The mystery of Rilloby Fair!" said Diana. "It would be exciting if we could solve it."

Barney went back to the fair reluctantly that evening. Miranda had enjoyed her day as much as he had. "Goodbye," he said. "I'll see you on Tuesday – if I can get over here. The fair leaves on Wednesday, you know, and I certainly shan't go with it. I don't want to work for Tonnerre."

"What will you do then, Barney?" asked Diana.

"Oh, I'll get another job somewhere," said Barney. "But I'll keep in touch with you. I'll send you a card telling you where I am always. And perhaps I shall be able to get a job somewhere near here when the summer holidays come."

He went off. The children all went to bed, feeling tired. "Though I can't imagine why," said Snubby. "We simply haven't done a thing today – not even taken poor old Loony for a walk."

"Woof," said Loony hopefully. But there was no walk that night!

The next day Great-uncle announced that he was going to Marloes Castle to arrange to pack up the valuable papers there, in order that they might be locked away in safety.

"I shall go about three o'clock," he said. "And seeing that Diana here has such an interest in old documents, I'd be glad to take her with me. She would be a help, I'm sure."

Diana was horrified. What, spend ages listening to dry information about centuries-old papers that she couldn't even read – all alone with Great-uncle! She gazed round at Roger and Snubby in despair.

They looked back. Poor old Diana! How awful! Then a thought came into Roger's mind. It would be rather interesting to go to that room again and have a good look round. He might find a clue the police had missed. Anyway, it would be fun to see if there was any single place where the thief could have come in.

"It's just conceivable there might be a secret passage somewhere," thought Roger. "I never thought of that!"

He pictured himself tapping round the wall of the room. He could have a look at the fireplace too, and see if it really was big enough for, say, Tonnerre.

"Great-uncle, I should like to come too," he said politely.

"So should I," said Snubby. "I'd awfully like to have a look round the grounds, Great-uncle. Do you think Lord Marloes would mind?"

"Dear me – so you would all like to keep me company this afternoon?" Great-uncle beamed at them, pleased at finding himself so popular all of a sudden. "Very well. I will certainly take you. I see no harm in your looking round the grounds, Snubby, if you behave yourself."

He said nothing about Loony and neither did Snubby. But when Snubby heard that Great-uncle was going in a car he knew there was no hope for Loony.

"I'd like a walk, Great-uncle," he said, "so if it's all right with you I'll walk across the fields and join you at the gates."

"Certainly, my boy, certainly," said Great-uncle. "Anything you like! We'll have a grand time together!"

"We shall have to be back in good time for supper," said Snubby suddenly. "There'll be meringues."

"How do you know?" asked Diana.

"Mrs Harris told me. She wouldn't eat her Sunday hat yesterday, though I begged and begged her to – so we're eating meringues tonight instead."

Mrs Lynton looked astonished. "What's all this about Mrs Harris's Sunday hat? Oh, Snubby, you haven't been upsetting Mrs Harris finding fault with her Sunday hat, surely?"

"Aunt Susan! She's got a marvellous Sunday hat," said Snubby indignantly. "It's got three roses, a wreath of violets, and five carnations in it. It's brilliant. I can quite well understand why she doesn't want to eat it."

"There are times when I think you are not quite sane, Snubby," said Mrs Lynton. "I don't know what your masters at school think of you."

"Oh, they think the same as you," Snubby assured her cheerfully. "I don't mind. It's all the same to me."

That afternoon the car came for Great-uncle, and he and Diana and Roger got into it. Snubby had already gone off with Loony. He was to meet them at the gates.

"Now for a nice happy afternoon," said Great-uncle, pleased. "Nothing I like better than browsing among old, rare papers, breathing in the air of past centuries. What a peaceful place that old room is."

It wasn't going to be. It was going to be just about the most exciting place in Rilloby that afternoon. But Great-uncle Robert didn't know that!

28

Things Begin to Happen

Snubby met them at the castle gates with Loony. Great-uncle eyed the spaniel with annoyance.

"I didn't say you could bring that dog!"

"You didn't say I wasn't to," pointed out Snubby in a reasonable voice. "Stop scratching, Loony. You do seem to have a bad effect on Loony, Great-uncle. It seems as if he's got to scratch whenever he sees you."

"You can't bring him into the castle," said Great-uncle determined not to enter into a conversation about scratching again. "You'll have to stay out here in the grounds."

Snubby didn't mind. He meant to explore the grounds thoroughly and see if he could find any clues. He also meant to find the dell where the stuffed animals had been again, and enjoy remembering that terrifying episode. He wondered if the sacks were still up on the wall. And what about the rope-ladder? Was it still under the bush?

"I expect it's there still – and the sacks too," he thought. "The police said nothing about those. Gosh, they're not very bright. I'd have spotted those at once if I'd been one of the police on the job."

Great-uncle presented his pass. He and Diana and Roger were taken into the castle, while Snubby wandered off into the grounds with an excited Loony, who foresaw all kinds of rabbit adventures for himself that afternoon.

Roger was impatient to be inside the room with the double-locked door. The butler unlocked one door, then the second one, and finally the third one, with its two keys. They then were in the old room, with its shelves of yellowed papers.

Roger and Diana glanced round with interest. Half the stuffed animals were gone, of course. The police had not brought them back. They were probably still somewhere in the police station, staring at the policemen with their lifeless, glassy eyes.

"All the big animals are left," said Roger, "I suppose the thief couldn't manage them. The squirrels are gone – and the fox-cubs, but not the foxes, and the pole-cat, and the albino badger. He wasn't very big either."

"Diana – we'll just go carefully through all the papers before we pack them," said Great-uncle, longing to explain pages upon pages to poor Diana. "Now this one . . ."

Diana cast a look of misery at Roger and went to listen. Roger began to look around. He examined the windows. Nobody could possibly undo those fastenings from outside! And only the very smallest, thinnest person could squeeze through the bars.

He went to the double-locked door and examined that. No thief could come in that way without keys – and if he had the keys, the burglar alarm would ring as soon as the door was opened. No – that way was impossible too.

He went to the fireplace. It was an old-fashioned open grate. As the fire was never used, there were no fire-irons at all, but only an old firescreen made of wrought-iron.

Roger bent down and tried to look up the chimney. It looked decidedly narrow. "I might be able to squeeze up," thought Roger. "But I doubt it – and it would be frightfully uncomfortable. I dare say it widens out a bit above though."

He looked at the fireplace itself. It was full of bits and pieces that had fallen down the chimney. "Of course, they might have been dislodged by somebody getting down, but on the other hand, bits and pieces always do fall down chimneys," thought Roger, feeling rather like a detective.

He went to the window and looked out. He saw something that filled him with extreme amazement! He stared intently.

Then a shout came to his ears.

"I say! Look at this!" cried Roger suddenly, making Diana and Great-uncle jump violently. "What's going on down there?"

He might well ask. Snubby, down in the grounds, was also feeling extremely astonished. He had been wandering round with Loony and had come to the little dell where he had seen the stuffed animals, when he heard a sound nearby.

He had turned – and looking down at him from out of the bushes was a hairy, grinning face with shining eyes! Snubby got a frightful shock. He thought it was one of the stuffed animals come to life!

"Gosh – what is it?" he said, and took a step backwards. Loony gave a delighted bark and rushed into the bushes where the hairy face was. Snubby was amazed. Loony should have barked or growled! Instead of that he had yelped in delight and gone off with the face!

Then Snubby heard yells and recognised Barney's voice. "Come here, you pest, you! Do you hear! Where have you gone?"

"It's Barney! What's he doing here?" said Snubby, full of surprise. "Loony, where have you gone? Hey, Barney, where are you?"

Barney's voice came back, surprised. "That you, Snubby? What are you doing here? I say, have you seen Burly? He's gone completely mad, so look out."

"Burly!" said Snubby, more amazed than ever. "What's he here for? Gosh, yes, I've seen him. At least, I saw his grinning face. He's gone now, and taken Loony with him."

He made his way towards Barney's voice. Barney was on the road side of the wall. He called again.

"I'm going to see if our rope-ladder is still under the bush, and the sacks on the wall, if the police haven't found them! I'm coming over. I simply must find Burly. He's gone crackers."

He found the rope-ladder under the bush and soon had it up on the wall. He climbed it quickly and sat on the sacks. He looked all round to see if he could spot Burly.

"What happened to make Burly so mad?" asked Snubby. "Why did he come all the way here?"

"Don't ask me!" said Barney. "I was in Vosta's caravan with both chimps when bless me if Hurly didn't pull out a pair of green gloves from under the blankets of his bunk."

"What – the ones we saw?" said Snubby.

"I don't know. The police had those – but I wouldn't put it past Hurly to sneak them out of the Inspector's pocket," said Barney. "I bet that's what he did! Anyway, Burly snatched them and put them on and they fitted him marvellously. Like a glove, in fact! He kept stroking them and muttering to himself, and then he rapped at the cupboard where his toy animals are kept."

He stopped for breath, still keeping a look-out for Burly from the top of the wall.

"Well, I hadn't the key to his toy cupboard. Vosta's got that," said Barney. "So he couldn't have his little toy animals to play with. Then he just seemed to go mad! He banged himself with his arms, and yowled like anything. And then he was out of the window like a streak, haring over the fair field!"

"Gosh!" said Snubby, enthralled with this story. "Go on!"

"Well, I followed him, of course," said Barney. "And he came straight here. I couldn't catch him up. He was up and over the wall as easy as anything – he didn't need a ladder. Well, I suppose he's somewhere in the grounds. What's made him come here?"

Before Snubby could answer a deep voice spoke from the other side of the wall. "I'm afraid I shall have to hold you for questioning concerning this ladder," said the voice. Barney almost fell off the wall.

"Golly – it's a copper," he said. "Where were you?"

"I've been hiding behind that tree ever since we found this ladder hidden, and the sacks on top of the wall," said the policeman. "We reckoned whoever put them there might use them again, if we didn't let on we'd found them. And seemingly we were right. You come down, and let me take you to the police station for questioning."

"No," said Barney, and scrambled down the other side as fast as he could. "I must find Burly," he said to the petrified Snubby. "And Miranda too. She scampered after him over the wall, and left me standing on the other side! Come on – take no notice of the copper. We can easily shake him off!"

He dragged poor Snubby into the bushes, while the annoyed policeman began to climb slowly and painfully up the rope-ladder. "Take me to the place where you saw Burly just now," said Barney. "He may still be near here."

Snubby took him to the dell – and sure enough, there was Burly, with Miranda and Loony! Burly was behaving in a peculiar fashion. His head held in his hands, he was rocking to and fro, making a little whimpering noise.

Miranda was stroking him, and Loony was licking him. It was plain that the chimpanzee was very unhappy.

He looked extremely peculiar in his red shorts, red-striped jersey – and green gloves! What was the matter with him? Why was he behaving like that?

Burly suddenly sprang up. He gave a loud howl and bounded away. Loony ran after him and Miranda ran too, whimpering. Both the animals knew that something was wrong with Burly.

Burly ran through the trees to the castle walls. Barney gave a shout. "Hey, Burly, come back! Come to old Barney!"

That was the shout that Roger had heard up in the old room on the second floor. He looked out and saw Burly tearing over to the castle, with his green gloves on, and behind him came Loony and Miranda, followed at some distance by Barney and Snubby – and behind them, good gracious, a policeman!

No wonder Roger could hardly believe his eyes. But what was to come was even more unbelievable.

Burly came to the walls of the castle. He leaped to a windowsill. He leaped to the drainpipe and shinned up it rapidly and easily. He leaped to another windowsill, and up another pipe. Then he climbed confidently up the thick ivy nearby, right to the roof.

"Look at that," said Snubby, awed. "What a climb. It was Burly I saw the other night! I'm sure it was!"

Burly was now on the roof. He ran to the one and only chimney and peered down it. He leaped into it and disappeared.

Down in the room below three startled people stared at one another. Great-uncle, Roger and Diana had tried in vain to see what was happening outside. They had lost sight of Burly when he had begun to climb up the walls – and then had caught a quick glimpse of him again as he leaped on to their windowsill and off. What in the world was he doing?

They heard a noise in the chimney. Roger ran to it. Two hairy legs appeared, and then Burly swung himself down into the fireplace, blinking. He had managed it easily.

He stood there, looking at three amazed people. Diana spoke to him. "Burly! What are you doing?"

Ah! That was the kind girl who had given

him a toy dog. Burly was no longer frightened to see people staring at him. He came out into the room, looking very strange in his extraordinary clothing.

Great-uncle shrank back. He had never seen Burly before. To him the chimpanzee looked fierce and savage. He was horrified to see Diana go up and take the green gloved hand. Suppose the creature bit her?

But Burly didn't bite. He stroked Diana's arm, and then he looked round the room. He sniffed the air. He ran to the shelves where the yellowed parchments were.

The three watched him, amazed. What was he doing now? Burly smelled each pile. He stopped at one and took out a paper. He sniffed another lot, and took another piece of parchment. Great-uncle watched him, gaping.

Roger touched Diana's arm. "The solution of the mystery!" he said. "I see it all now. How could we have been so blind?"

29

Burly Is Very Clever

All three watched the chimpanzee as he sniffed through the papers and took one here and one there. He seemed quite certain which to take. There was no hesitation at all.

"How does he know which to choose?" said Great-uncle Robert, puzzled. "He's taking one or two of the most valuable – I can see that. But how does he know?"

"He sniffs before he pulls a paper out of its pile," said Diana. "Look, each time, he sniffs first."

"Well! Of course! I know how he knows which papers to take!" exclaimed Roger suddenly. "Diana – do you remember that hairy man – how we watched him sliding his magnifying glass up and down some of the papers?"

"Yes, I remember," said Diana.

"Well, he must have had something on the base of the magnifying-glass that was rubbed off on the papers," said Roger excitedly. "And the stuff would leave a smell – and when the chimp was sent to take certain papers he knew which to take because of the smell. See him sniffing at them all now!"

"Remarkable. Most remarkable," said Great-uncle, who looked rather dazed. "I suppose he's trained to do that. Chimpanzees must be extremely clever."

"Oh, they are," said Roger, watching Burly take yet another paper. "But that's an old circus trick, Great-uncle, to smear papers with something that smells, so that an animal will instinctively choose those. Who trained you, Burly?"

Burly looked up at his name and gabbled something. His green-gloved hands worked quickly through the parchments.

"No fingerprints, you see – not even a chimp's prints left behind!" said Roger. "I wonder what made him come along here this afternoon to do the job he should really have done the other night?"

"Perhaps he saw the gloves and they reminded him," suggested Diana. "Oh – what's he going to do now?"

Burly had caught sight of the stuffed animals. He dropped all his papers on the floor and whimpered. He ran across to the few animals left and lifted up a fox. Great-uncle quietly gathered up the papers, opened a drawer in the nearby table, and put them inside. He meant to have them examined to see exactly what gave them the smell that Burly recognised so easily.

The chimpanzee sat down on the floor and cuddled the stuffed fox. Diana nudged Roger.

"I'm sure I know what happened the other night," she whispered. "He came for the papers with no other idea in his head but to do the sort of job he's often done before, and he must suddenly have seen the stuffed animals staring at him in the moonlight! You know how mad he is on toy animals. He must have thought these stuffed ones were extra big toy ones – possibly put there for him!"

"Yes, and he took them into the grounds, one after the other – just the little ones that he could manage easily," went on Roger. "Poor Burly. He stood them all in the dell, and for some reason left them there. But he didn't take any of the papers. He was so wrapped up in the animals."

"And I expect that's why the chimps were so miserable the next day when we saw them," said Diana. "Somebody had scolded Burly hard – and he was upset, so Hurly was upset too. Do you remember how they sat with their arms round one another, looking thoroughly miserable?"

"Who had scolded them?" wondered Roger. "Vosta, do you suppose?"

"Maybe. And probably Tonnerre too, because Vosta said he had, you remember?" said Diana. "Somehow or other Tonnerre's in this mystery, Roger. I'm sure he is!"

Burly put down the fox and picked up a stuffed dog, very moth-eaten indeed. He cuddled that too. Then he got up and looked at the fireplace, evidently considering whether or not he could get up the chimney with such a large animal.

There suddenly came the sound of doors being unlocked. Voices were heard. Burly looked alarmed. He ran to Diana and crouched down beside her, chattering. She patted him gently on the head. "Don't be afraid, Burly. I won't let anyone hurt you!"

The door of the room was unlocked with its two separate keys. It opened. In poured

Barney, Snubby, Miranda, Loony, the policeman, the custodian and the butler!

"Is Burly here? He went down the chimney!" cried Snubby.

"Yes – there he is!" cried Barney and ran to the chimpanzee, who took his hand trustingly. He loved Barney. Miranda leaped on to the chimpanzee's shoulder, chattering. He looked happier at once.

The policeman looked absolutely bewildered. What with cheeky boys, a spaniel and a monkey, and now a chimpanzee, he didn't really know what to do. He looked with relief at Great-uncle, glad to see a responsible looking grown-up.

"Perhaps you can help me, sir," he said. "What's all this about?"

"Constable – we have found the one who stole the stuffed animals," said Great-uncle solemnly. "Before our very eyes this afternoon he stole more valuable papers."

"Then I shall arrest him," said the constable at once, importantly. "Which of them is it, sir?"

"It's the chimpanzee," said Great-uncle. "Be careful how you arrest him!"

Snubby gave a chortle at the sight of the policeman's alarmed face. Loony sat down and began to scratch himself violently. Burly put down the stuffed dog he was hugging and took Miranda into his arms instead, cuddling her and crooning.

"Hrrm, I find that beast rather pathetic," said Great-uncle unexpectedly. "Can't blame him for anything he's done, Constable. Whoever trained him is responsible. That's the fellow you want – the trainer."

Heavy footsteps came down the little passage to the door, and in came the Inspector. The policeman had telephoned for him as soon as he had got into the castle, and he had jumped into his car and come along at once.

"Well," he said, looking round at the big company in amazement. "You're a mixed lot, I must say. My word – the green gloves! Look who's wearing them! Well, well, well!"

He stared at Burly as if he couldn't believe his eyes. The chimpanzee stared back. He remembered the Inspector. This was the man out of whose pocket Hurly had taken the green gloves. He took them off suddenly and flung them on the floor.

The constable began to talk to the Inspector, trying to tell him what had happened, but Barney interrupted. "I can tell you all that happened, sir," he said. "I can see it all now! I understand why the sight of the gloves sent Burly here again. I understand why . . ."

"Speak when you're spoken to," said the Inspector. He turned to Great-uncle Robert. "Mr Grey, perhaps you would say a few words first. I'm all at sea."

Somehow or other, first by this person and then by that, he was told every single thing. He listened, astonished and almost disbelieving. He was shown the fireplace where Burly had come down. He was shown the pile of papers that Burly had so carefully chosen after sniffing them. He sniffed at them too.

"I can smell something myself," he said, sniffing again. "Yes – a very clever trick. The chimp had no other way of telling which were the valuable papers and which weren't, except by smell. There's somebody remarkably clever behind all this. Who is it?"

Everyone took a turn at sniffing at the papers. Certainly they had a faint, elusive smell, quite distinguishable.

"So that's how the other thefts were planned," said the Inspector thoughtfully. "Someone examined the collections first, and smeared the papers he wanted with something to make them smell. He must also have examined how the chimp could get in and out – a skylight sometimes, a chimney another time, a small window a third time, or maybe a ventilator – somewhere impossible for a grown man to get through. But the chimp could always manage to climb and wriggle through a tiny entrance – he's small and supple and a born acrobat."

"A most remarkable and successful plan,"

put in Great-uncle. "If we could only lay our hands on the hairy man who was here the other day smearing the papers with something on the base of his large magnifying-glass – you'd have the ring-leader, Inspector."

"Yes," said Barney. "But there must be two or three go-betweens, Inspector, Vosta must be one. He'd have to take Burly to whatever place had been chosen and point out the way to go up the walls. And there must be another go-between too – the one who warns Vosta what to do – the one who received the note we found a bit of the other day – that said 'Marloes Castle. Midnight'. Who received that note?"

"Quite a lot of loose ends to tie up!" said the Inspector. "Well, we'll see if we can tie up a few today. We'll take the chimp back to the fair and find out where Vosta is – he may be back by this time."

The custodian and the butler, neither of whom had said a single word, so completely amazed and bewildered were they, let the little company out of the castle. The Inspector took the pile of papers with him that Burly had so carefully chosen. Burly went down the stairs holding Barney's hand, chattering away to him.

Two cars stood outside – the Inspector's and the one that Great-uncle had hired. "Room for everyone," said the Inspector genially. "Hop in. We'll all go to the fair. Take the chimp, the monkey and the dog into the other car, if you don't mind. Now – are we all set? To the fair then!"

30

The Mystery Is Solved

Vosta was back in his caravan, puzzled to find Burly gone, when they all arrived in the field. He looked frightened when he saw the Inspector. Burly ran to him and flung his arms round him.

"What have you been up to?" said Vosta to Burly. "And where have *you* been?" he said to Barney. "I told you not to leave the chimps."

"Illia Juan Vosta, I have some questions to ask you, and I must warn you that anything you say may be taken down and used in evidence against you," said the Inspector sternly. The constable took out a black notebook and licked his pencil, preparing to write.

Vosta looked extremely alarmed. "I haven't done anything," he stammered.

"You have trained this chimpanzee to steal, and to break into various buildings," went on the Inspector in a cold, calm voice. "We know that various papers are smeared with a substance that the chimpanzee can smell, and these are the papers he takes. We know further that . . ."

"I didn't have anything to do with that," cried out Vosta, turning very pale. "I've always said it was a mug's game, using the chimp. I've never had anything to do with it."

"Except that you lent your chimpanzee, which you yourself had trained to steal, and you took him each time to the place where the theft was to be committed," said the Inspector in a voice that sent a shiver down Snubby's back. "Didn't you, Vosta?"

"They're not my chimps," muttered Vosta. "And I never trained them to steal. They were trained before I had them."

"Whose were they before you had them?" rapped out the Inspector.

Vosta looked terrified. "They were Tonnerre's," he said in a low voice. "He trained them. He trained Hurly to pick pockets, and he trained Burly to do all kinds of other stealing tricks. Burly's clever. You can teach him anything."

"Why did you take on the chimpanzees from Tonnerre?" asked the Inspector.

"I was an acrobat," said Vosta, still in a low voice. "And I hurt my back. So Tonnerre offered me the chimps if I'd keep on with him in the fair – and do one or two things he wanted."

"I see. And one of the things he wanted was that you should take Burly to whatever building he told you, and see that he got in somehow and sniffed out the papers he had marked," said the Inspector.

"*He* never marked them," said Vosta. "He didn't know a thing about old papers. I used to take them from Burly and give them to Tonnerre and he passed them on to someone else. I don't know who – but it was the fellow who did the marking of the papers. This fellow used to tell Tonnerre where to take the fair – we never knew where we were going."

"Quite. I imagine he chose whatever place he had marked down for his next theft," said the Inspector. "And now just tell me the name of the man at the top of all this."

"I tell you, I don't know," said Vosta obstinately. "Why don't you ask Tonnerre? Why pick on me? I'm only the cat's-paw."

"It's the hairy man," said Snubby, butting in. "We do know that – do you know a very hairy man, Vosta?"

"I'm not answering any questions from you," snarled Vosta. "If you kids hadn't come here, snooping and prying—"

"That's enough, Vosta," said the Inspector. "Constable, stay here with him. I'm going across to this fellow Tonnerre. He, too, is only a cat's-paw, it seems, but a bigger one than Vosta. Still, maybe he'll be able to lead us to the real villain."

Barney led him to Tonnerre's caravan. The fair folk, who had stood around in silence, watching Vosta being interviewed, moved back.

Old Ma called out: "Tonnerre's got a visitor. He's in a black mood. You've got to watch out, Mister!"

The Inspector did not deign to reply. He rapped imperiously on the door of Tonnerre's caravan.

"Go away!" yelled Tonnerre's voice. "Didn't I say I wasn't to be disturbed?"

"Open up," came the Inspector's stern voice. The door was flung open and Tonnerre stood there, frowning blackly. He shut the door behind him and came down the steps.

"Say what you've got to say and go," he growled.

"Who's your visitor, Tonnerre?" asked the Inspector mildly. "Let's have a look at him."

"He's a gentleman, see? I'm not going to have him dragged into any funny business," said Tonnerre angrily. "He's a friend of mine, with nothing to do with you at all. Anyway, what's brought you here again, wasting my time and interfering?"

"Let's have a look at your visitor, Tonnerre," repeated the Inspector. "What are you hiding him away for?"

Snubby was so full of excitement and

anticipation that he could hardly contain himself. His enemy has met his match! The Inspector wouldn't take no for an answer. Who was the visitor?

"I bet it's the hairy man. I bet it is," said Snubby to himself. "He's come to get the papers and he's wild with Tonnerre because the chimp didn't get them."

Tonnerre made no move to open the door but it suddenly opened behind him and somebody came out on to the top step.

"What is all this disturbance?" said a cultured voice. "Tonnerre, have I come at an awkward moment? I will go."

He stepped down, but the Inspector placed himself in front of him. "Your name, sir?" he asked.

The four children gazed at the man in disappointment. He was not the hairy man. He was quite clean-shaven. He had smooth black hair tinged with grey, no moustache, no shaggy eyebrows, no beard.

"My name is Thomas Colville," said the man. "My business with Mr Tonnerre is private – he and I are old friends. I am sorry to see he seems to be in trouble. My business with him can wait."

"You didn't happen to come and see him about some papers you wanted him to get for you, did you?" said the Inspector stolidly.

"I don't know what you are talking

about, my good fellow," said the man, and pushed by the Inspector impatiently.

Snubby stared at him. No, he certainly wasn't a bit like the hairy man – though he was about the same size and build.

Snubby walked a few steps beside the man, staring at him, much to his annoyance. Then Snubby suddenly gave such a yell that Loony barked wildly and ran to him.

"I say – he *is* the man we saw looking at the papers – the hairy man. He *is*! I couldn't help noticing the tremendous tufts of hair he had growing out of his ears – and look, he's got them, just the same. It's him!"

Things happened all at once then. The man began to run. The constable, watching from Vosta's caravan, saw him, and ran to cut him off. Young Un ran out and tripped him up neatly. Tonnerre went mad and tried to hit the Inspector. Loony bit him and then everyone closed in, yelling and shrieking with excitement, so that the poor Inspector didn't know what was going on for a few minutes.

"You take your sister and brother home," he said urgently to Roger. He thought that Snubby was Roger's brother. "Go on – we may be going to have a rough time here. We'll get the police station to send up men quickly."

Roger fled with Diana, Snubby and Loony. He was sorry to go at such a time,

but he knew they should go in case things began to get too rough.

Outside the gate stood two cars – one was the police car, with Great-uncle Robert waiting patiently inside, rather alarmed at the excitement going on in the fair field. The other was the taxi he had hired, complete with its driver.

"Oh, good!" said Roger, stopping. "I'd forgotten the cars and Great-uncle. I say, Great-uncle, things are boiling up terrifically – everything's really smashing – and the police station is sending more men."

"Bless us all!" said poor Great-uncle in alarm, and clambered out of the police car as quickly as he could. He got into the taxi and in a quavering voice told the man to drive home.

"I must get home," the old man kept saying. "This isn't good for my heart. Dear, dear – little did I think I'd get mixed up with a lot of criminals and madmen and chimpanzees when I came to stay with your mother. I must go. I must leave. I can't stay a night longer!"

"But Great-uncle – it's been absolutely great," protested Snubby. "I mean – if you want a first-class mystery, well, you couldn't have a better one than the one to do with Rilloby Fair."

But Great-uncle didn't want any mysteries or adventures. "I just want to pack my things and go," he said. "That man Tonnerre's a dreadful fellow – I was glad I was safely in the car when I saw him come down the caravan steps as black as – as –"

"Thunder," said Diana.

"He looked as if he might be the chief of some horrible gang," shuddered poor Great-uncle.

"The Green Hands Gang," said Snubby, with a chortle.

31

All's Well!

Great-uncle was as good as his word. As soon as he got in, he found Mrs Lynton, announced his intention of leaving that very night, and went up to pack his bag.

Mrs Lynton was amazed. She looked at the excited children.

"What's the matter with him? What have you been doing?"

"Nothing!" said Roger indignantly. "Oh, Mum, do listen – we've got the most exciting news."

"Well, here's your father – tell him too," said his mother. "And do come in to your dinner. You're so dreadfully late, and Mrs Harris has made you some meringues for your pudding."

"Gosh – do you know we've never had any tea?" said Snubby in an injured voice. "Would you believe it? No wonder I feel so hungry."

"So many things have been happening that it's difficult to know where to begin our story," said Roger to his mother.

"Go and wash before you begin," said his mother, suddenly noticing how dirty they all looked. "Your news can wait. It can't be as important and exciting as all that."

But it was, of course – and when the three children were at last sitting down to eat an enormous meal, the two grown-ups gaped in astonishment when told the extra-ordinary tale.

"You should have seen the chimp going at top speed up the wall!" said Snubby, waving his fork.

"You should have seen him coming down the chimney!" said Roger, getting out of the way of Snubby's fork.

"You should have seen him sniffing at the papers to see which to take!" said Diana.

It was a very disturbed evening. Great-uncle condescended to have some dinner, when he had packed his bag, and he too added his quota to the tale. The Inspector arrived to make his report. Lord Marloes telephoned to Great-uncle to ask for details of the latest excitement at the castle, and asked him to be his guest in town. Great-uncle then telephoned for a taxi.

"I'm really very sorry you've had such an upsetting stay," said Mrs Lynton. "Certainly you seemed to be as much in the thick of things as anyone else, Uncle Robert. Say goodbye, children!"

The three stood at the gate and shouted goodbye. The last that Great-uncle saw of them was Snubby holding Loony in his arms, making him wave his paw violently.

"That dog!" said Great-uncle Robert, sinking back into the taxi. "Well, thank goodness he can't sit down and scratch himself in front of me any more!"

And then Barney arrived. He whistled outside the window, standing half-hidden in the darkness.

"There's Barney!" said Snubby, almost falling from his chair in his anxiety to get to the window.

"Ask him in," said Mrs Lynton. "We might as well hear his tale too. I never did know such a set of children for getting into all kinds of trouble!"

"Come in, Barney!" yelled Snubby, and Loony raced out of the room into the garden, barking madly. Barney came in looking rather pale and worried.

Miranda was on his shoulder as usual, and she chattered merrily when she saw the friends she knew. She leaped off Barney's shoulder on to Snubby's.

"Don't let her come too near me," said Mrs Lynton in alarm. "I do like her – but I really can't bear monkeys."

"I'll stick her inside my shirt," said Snubby. "She's cold."

Miranda disappeared from view for a

while. Loony went and sniffed at Snubby's shirt. He felt a little jealous to think Miranda was so close to his beloved master.

"What happened when we left, Barney?" asked Roger. "Did everything blow up?"

"Pretty well," said Barney. "Tonnerre's been taken off, and so has Vosta. I hear they're not coming back, so I don't know if that means they've gone to prison."

"They haven't taken Hurly and Burly to prison, have they?" asked Snubby in alarm.

"Of course not," said Barney. "Billy Tell's taking care of them. I offered to, but the show-folk say they don't want me there any more. They say I put the police on to Tonnerre and Vosta."

"But you didn't!" cried all three children indignantly. "You didn't!"

"Well, they think I did," said Barney. "So I've been chucked out. And Miranda too. The fair's breaking up tomorrow, and everyone's going here, there and everywhere. But nobody wants me to go with them."

"What – was even Young Un horrid – and Old Ma?" asked Snubby amazed.

"Young Un's all right but he's got to do what the others do," said Barney. "Show-folk don't like the police – and if they think somebody's split on them they chuck them out."

"It's not fair," said Diana, almost in tears. "It wasn't your fault that Tonnerre and

Vosta and the hairy man got caught. So they should be too."

"What happened to the hairy man?" asked Roger. "Was he taken off too?"

"Yes. He's the big man behind all these planned thefts," said Barney. "He paid Tonnerre to arrange with Vosta for the chimp to steal the papers he wanted. Well, I'm glad Tonnerre's gone. He was a black-hearted fellow."

"That's what Old Ma said," put in Roger. "Well, Barney, what are you going to do? Where are you going to sleep tonight?"

"It's a fine night," said Barney. "I'm sleeping in a barn not far off. The farmer said I could."

"Oh no you're not," said Mrs Lynton suddenly, entering into the conversation.

Barney looked at her in surprise. The children stared too. They had forgotten that she was in the room, sewing.

"Great-uncle's left tonight," said Mrs Lynton. "So we've got a guest-room again. If Diana likes to give me a hand, I'll have the bed made up for Barney. He can stay with you till you have to go back to school – and by that time perhaps we shall have found a job for him."

Barney was quite overcome. "It's very good of you," he began, but he couldn't finish because Snubby swept by him and almost knocked him over. He flung his arms

round his aunt's neck and hugged her like a bear.

"Aunt Susan! I kept saying to myself, 'Say Barney can stay!' and you said it."

"Oh, don't be so ridiculous, dear," said his aunt, "and stop strangling me. It was nothing to do with your willing me – I made up my mind to ask Barney as soon as I saw your Great-uncle off in the car."

Barney's face shone. "Why – I'll be here for about two weeks," he said. "Two whole weeks. But what about Miranda? You don't like monkeys, Mrs Lynton."

"Oh, I can put up with Miranda so long

as she doesn't leap on to my shoulder," said Mrs Lynton bravely. "I dare say I shall get used to monkeys if she comes to stay. After all, I've got used to Loony, and I really didn't think I'd ever do that!"

"Woof!" said Loony, hearing his name mentioned. He hadn't stopped watching the lump inside Snubby's shirt, which meant that Miranda was still curled up there.

"It will be lovely," said Diana, thinking of the two weeks ahead. "There'll be us four – and Miranda – and Loony . . ."

"And Sardine," said Roger, seeing the big black cat coming softly in, eyeing Loony in a way that meant she was just about to spring on him. "Yes – we'll have a super time."

"And a peaceful time, I hope," said Mrs Lynton, getting up to go and make Barney's bed. "It's all been much too exciting for me."

"Oh, Mum – I loved the Rilloby Fair mystery!" said Roger. "Every minute of it. I'd like it all over again."

"No – another one would be better still," said Snubby, tickling Miranda under his shirt. "I'd like another mystery, as good as this – and we'll have one too! Won't we, Loony?"

"Woof," said Loony, and jumped up to sniff at Miranda. She put out a tiny paw and pulled his ear.

"Well, as long as you four and Miranda and Loony are together, you're sure to get into plenty of trouble!" said Mrs Lynton. "But spare me a mystery for a little while, will you? I haven't got over this one yet!"

"Right," promised Snubby generously. "We'll give you a bit of a rest, Aunt Susan – and then whoosh, we'll be heading into another mystery – the biggest one that ever was!"

Enid Blyton

THE BARNEY MYSTERIES

Join Barney, Roger, Diana and Snubby
on their mystery-solving adventures!

ISBN 978-1-84135-728-7

ISBN 978-1-84135-729-4

ISBN 978-1-84135-730-0

ISBN 978-1-84135-731-7

ISBN 978-1-84135-732-4

ISBN 978-1-84135-733-1

Enid Blyton

THE ADVENTUROUS FOUR

Follow the adventures of Tom, twins Pippa
and Zoe, and their friend Andy who has a sailing
boat on which the four love to go exploring.

ISBN 978-1-84135-734-8

ISBN 978-1-84135-735-5

ISBN 978-1-84135-736-2

Enid Blyton

The Secret Series

Follow the adventures of Mike, Peggy and
Nora as they discover a secret island, explore
the heart of Africa and unravel the mysteries of
the Killimooin Mountains...

PB ISBN 978-1-84135-673-0
HB ISBN 978-1-84135-748-5

PB ISBN 978-1-84135-675-4
HB ISBN 978-1-84135-749-2

PB ISBN 978-1-84135-676-1
HB ISBN 978-1-84135-750-8

PB ISBN 978-1-84135-677-8
HB ISBN 978-1-84135-751-5

PB ISBN 978-1-84135-674-7
HB ISBN 978-1-84135-752-2

PB ISBN 978-1-84135-678-5
HB ISBN 978-1-84135-753-9

Enid Blyton

Enid Blyton was born in London in 1897. Her childhood was spent in Beckenham, Kent and as a child she began to write poems, stories and plays.

She trained as a teacher, but devoted most of her life to writing for children. Her first book was a collection of poems, published in 1922. In 1926 she began to write a weekly magazine for children called *Sunny Stories*, and it was here that many of her most popular stories and characters first appeared.

She wrote more than 700 books for children, many of which have been translated into over 30 languages.